BLOOD BANE TOWER

AN IAN DEX SUPERNATURAL THRILLER BOOK 3

JOHN P. LOGSDON

CHRISTOPHER P. YOUNG

CRIMSON MYTH
PRESS

Thanks to TEAM ASS!
Advanced Story Squad

This is the first line of readers of the series. Their job is to help me keep things in check and also to make sure I'm not doing anything way off base in the various story locations!

(listed in alphabetical order by first name)

Bennah Phelps
Cassandra Hall
Hal Bass
John Debnam
Larry Diaz Tushman
Marie McCraney
Mike Helas
Natalie Fallon
Noah Sturdevant
Paulette Kilgore
Penny Campbell-Myhill
Soobee Dewson

Thanks to Team DAMN
Demented And Magnificently Naughty

This crew is the second line of readers who get the final draft of the story, report any issues they find, and do their best to inflate my fragile ego.

(listed in alphabetical order by first name)

Adam Goldstein, Adam Saunders-Pederick, Allen Stark, Amy Robertson, Andrew Greeson, Bennah Phelps, Bob Topping, Bonnie Dale Keck, Carmen Romano, Carol Howcroft, Carolyn Fielding, Carolyn Jean Evans, Charlotte Webby, Debbie Tily, Denise King, Hal Bass, Ian Nick Tarry, Jacky Oxley, Jamie Gray, Jan Gray, Jodie Stackowiak, John Debnam, Kate Smith, Kathleen Portig, Kathryne Nield, Larry Diaz Tushman, Laura Stoddart, Lyn Mason, Marie McCraney, Mark Beech, Mark Brown, MaryAnn Sims, Matthew Stuart Thomas Wilson, Megan McBrien, Mike Helas, Natalie Fallon, Noah Sturdevant, Patricia Wellfare, Paulette Kilgore, Ruth Nield, Sandee Lloyd, Scott Ackermann, Scott Reid, Stephen Bagwell, 'Toni Shepherd.

CHAPTER 1

I used to despise going to see Dr. Vernon, the psychiatrist for the Las Vegas Paranormal Police Department (PPD), but that changed today.

As I was lying back on the couch going over the details of the last mission, describing how that old fart, Shitfaced Fred, had built up an army of zombies bent on attacking the Strip, a shadow fell over me.

I looked up and saw Dr. Vernon's amethyst eyes staring down at me hungrily.

She'd taken off her glasses and her hair hung along the sides of her dark-skinned cheeks. She was unbuttoning her blouse, which caused me to stop telling her about the mission.

"Don't stop," she said in a sultry way. "Tell me more."

"Telling you about zombies is turning you on?"

She paused and squinted at me. "No. Hearing about how you take matters into your own hands does."

"Oh," I said as thoughts of *You should probably leave right about now* ran through my head. Unfortunately, thoughts of *You're not going anywhere, flyboy* ran through that piece of

1

anatomy that often controlled my patterns of thought. "The Admiral" seemed to do most of my thinking, after all. And, yes, that was the pet name I used for my junk, which was—interestingly—a name given to it by my partner on the force, Rachel Cress. This was before I was chief, of course.

"Tell me how you used your gun," Dr. Vernon whispered as she lowered herself onto my chest.

"Whoa," I said, pushing her away. "Couldn't you lose your license for this?"

She tilted her head. "Nope, but I appreciate your concern."

"Really? I thought that—"

"You're a supernatural, Ian. I'm a normal. My license only prohibits me from having relations with patients who are normals." She traced my face with her index finger. "My uncle is a friend of one of the Directors, which is why I work with the PPD. I do it as a favor. Well, that, and to collect a nice chunk of change on the side."

"So you can bone anyone on the PPD, even though you know our deepest, darkest secrets?" I was perplexed by this. "Don't you see that as a problem?"

"With most of your crew, yes. With you? No. You're never going to change your horndog status, and it's frankly not my job to try and help you change it either." She stopped her seductive play and pulled away slightly. "Unless you want me to help you change?"

"Not even a little bit."

"There you go." She nestled back into place. "I'm here to make sure you and your crew remain fit for duty. That's it. I'll help you resolve any internal issues in order to keep you ready for duty, too, of course, but I'm not trying to fix anything else."

"This is kind of...fantastic." I gave her a quick look. "We

still have that doctor-patient confidentiality deal, though, right?"

"Probably."

"Good enough for me!"

We started getting busy, when another thought struck. I pushed her away again.

"Wait, which Director is your uncle's friend?"

"EQK," she replied.

"He has friends?" I started, but her kissing interrupted my train of thought.

The Admiral had taken over and things were progressing quite nicely, when the word "time" came to mind.

It was the word that Gabe had said to me at the Three Angry Wives Pub. I remembered because he said it in a way that made it impossible for me to forget. This was the same thing he'd done to me with the word "flashes," where I ended up seeing a bunch of information about Shitfaced Fred. Turned out to have helped a lot when we'd reached our showdown, but the side effects of that *Flashes* thing rocked me to my core.

But why was I suddenly thinking about the *Time* word that he'd shared?

Even more pressing, why was I thinking about Gabe at all right now?

That was a question I'm sure Dr. Vernon would love to dig into further during one of our normal sessions.

Anyway, what did *Time* have to do with my current...

I smiled.

"What?" said the ravenous doctor as she continued her rhythmic motion.

I wasn't sure what *Time* was going to do, but I had a feeling it would either stop time or slow time. I hoped for the latter. There wasn't much I could think of that'd be sweeter than a one-hour orgasm, after all. Well, not in realtime, obviously. That would be horrible.

Time.

I thought the word in such a way that it clicked. I can't really describe it, other than to say it felt right when I thought it. Of course, Dr. Vernon had clearly been building up to a release, so not much felt *wrong* at the moment.

Everything slowed drastically.

I felt I could sit outside of the event I was currently in, acting at real speed while the world around me crawled at a snail's pace. But I wasn't interested in that at the moment. Instead, I allowed myself to wallow in intense pleasure for what seemed like eternity.

The look on Dr. Vernon's face was incredible. A mixture of desire and excitement. It was quite the turn on, but I managed to maintain my resolve.

The entire event likely only lasted about forty-five seconds, but it'd felt like fifteen minutes.

This *Time* thing was definitely going to be in the top-3 of my bedroom tricks going forward.

And that's when time resumed its normal pace, bringing us both back to the present. I didn't feel any ill effects from this *Time* thing, which was great considering what *Flashes* had done to me.

"That was amazing," she said, nearly breathless as she collapsed on my chest.

Moments later she resumed her ride-em-cowboy act with vigor.

Oh, yeah, going to see the shrink wasn't going to be nearly the chore anymore.

"Ian, honey," said Lydia, our Artificial Intelligence dispatcher, interrupting my fun time, "we have a problem."

Dr. Vernon couldn't hear Lydia because the voice came through my connector, a communications device implanted into the brains of all PPD officers. But *I* could hear the voice and that made things trying.

"I can't really talk right now," I replied without saying a word as Dr. Vernon kept going like a woman possessed. "We made some, uh, headway in this session, and now Dr. Vernon is *really* riding the point home."

"I know you're at your appointment, sugar plum, but we have a normal who is being held captive by a group of supers."

"Shit," I said aloud.

"What's the matter?" Dr. Vernon said, stopping her motion.

"Sorry," I said. "I was just talking to Lydia through my connector."

The good doctor winked. "That's kinky."

It was my turn to squint.

"Right, well, it seems that we have a normal in trouble," I said as she slowed down. "I might have to go."

"You're going to leave me like this?"

"Well, uh…" I gulped. "Lydia, are the other officers on their way?"

"Yes, sweetums."

"Great," I replied, all smiles, knowing that my team was more than equipped to handle any situation. "Tell them that I'll be there as soon as I can. I'm in the middle of someone… erm, *something* right now."

"Is everything okay, puddin'?" Lydia asked. "You sound distressed."

"Everything will be fine in about five more minutes," I answered.

Dr. Vernon's eyebrows shot up. "Only five?"

"Make that fifteen, Lydia."

CHAPTER 2

"Glad you could join us," said Rachel as I stepped out of my red Aston Martin. She then studied me for a second and shook her head. "Unbelievable."

"What?"

"You know what," she replied with much disdain.

I grinned uncontrollably. Of course I knew what she was talking about. She had the ability to spot whenever I'd gotten lucky. I don't know how she did this, but it was uncanny.

It was clear she did not approve, but she knew the depths of the side effects I dealt with from being an amalgamite with enhanced genetics. I was the horniest guy on the planet. At least that was the theory, seeing that I was the only known amalgamite on the planet, and definitely the only one who was also a PPD officer. *And* since I was in the PPD, my genetics were enhanced even further. Each tick in the plus column included one horniness point. That gave me a lot of horniness points.

"You did it with the doctor?"

I shrugged. "We had a breakthrough, in a manner of speaking."

"Ugh."

She looked away.

Rachel and I used to get busy with each other all the time. Honestly, she was everything a guy could hope for in a woman: beautiful, smart, snarky, amazing in the sack, and loyal. But that was the past. Ever since becoming her boss, our relationship became off-limits. Not that there was a ton of depth to our relationship before, but there could have been.

I sighed at the thought.

"Anyway, what's going on here?"

She pointed at a building that was a block away. It was small and dimly lit, which kind of fit in with this area of town. There looked to be armed goons walking around.

"Guards?"

"More like sentries," Rachel said. "Griff and Chuck are on the other side."

"Felicia and Jasmine?"

"Rooftop." She pointed again. "They've got Warren with them."

"Why?"

"I guess in case we need a wizard, Ian." It was said deadpan.

I could see why we'd want to have the mages onboard. Rachel, Griff, and Jasmine worked well together and they could get spells flying fast. But wizards were notoriously slow. By the time Warren got a jolt of naughtiness flying through the air, the battle would be over...assuming there *was* a battle forthcoming. Another glance at the sentries signaled that was a strong possibility.

"Griff," I said through the connector, "what's the status on your side?"

"We have ascertained the complement of sentries surrounding the building," he replied in his posh voice.

"There are eleven in total. Four are werewolves, five are vampires, and two are djinn."

"Swell."

"Charles and I believe there to be more on the interior of the building, however."

"Griff's right," Felecia chimed in. "Jasmine and I have spotted three already."

"Even better," I said with a sigh.

"Jasmine's working with Warren to cast a blinding spell at the dudes around the front," Felicia added. "Should only be another couple of minutes."

I gave Rachel a surprised look.

"That was fast," I said directly to her.

"You were late, remember?"

I cleared my throat.

It was often difficult to know if Rachel was annoyed at me or just playing the part of my conscience.

"What can I say?" I said. "The doctor had a prescription that I needed to…fill."

"I think I'm going to gag."

"That's what she said."

Her eyes iced over. "I don't doubt it."

"Nice." I sighed. "You're no fun anymore, you know that?"

There was no response.

"I thought you were all happy after spending time with those guys from the Little Rock Paranormal Police Department?" I scratched my chin for a second. "Cletus and Merle, right?"

She gave me a sidelong glare.

"No good?" I pressed.

"They were fine," she answered. "Can we keep our minds on the case, please?"

Touchy.

Well, there was no point in pushing the topic any further.

Obviously things hadn't worked out the way Rachel had planned. I'd be lying if I didn't say I'd been a bit jealous of Cletus and Merle at first. Again, my partner on the force was beyond hot. But things were what they were, so I allowed myself to be okay with it.

Rachel, though, clearly wasn't.

"Look," I said gently, "it's none of my business what went on between you two…erm…three." I coughed. "Anyway, I'm still your partner and that means I've got your back. So if you want to talk, I'll be nonjudgmental about it."

Her shoulders slumped. "For real?"

"Of course," I said, putting a hand on her shoulder. "That's what partners do, Rachel."

She stared into my eyes in such a way that I had the sense she was judging my true intentions. I had nothing nefarious up my sleeve, but I could understand why she may have thought that. The fact was that I was known to be somewhat of a douche from time to time.

"I couldn't do it," she admitted, looking away.

"Couldn't do what?" I asked.

"*It.*"

"The movie?"

"What?" She furrowed her brow. "No, not the movie, you idiot. I'm talking about Cletus and Merle. I didn't hook up with them."

"Oh." That was odd. I thought for sure she was ready to go to town with them both. At least it sure seemed that way when we were out wiping up zombies. "But I thought you—"

"So did I," she interrupted. "So did I."

"Then what happened?"

She shut her eyes and groaned, but before she could say a word, Felicia cut in.

"Warren's ready," she said. "Cover your eyes. The flash is going off in five seconds."

I pulled out my Desert Eagle .50 caliber that I lovingly called "Boomy" and got ready for action.

"We'll talk about this later," I said, shutting my eyes before the flash of light ensued.

"Or not," Rachel replied.

CHAPTER 3

The sentries yelled out as the flash hit the area. I couldn't blame them, seeing as though it felt like I got an instant tan from it—and I was down the street.

We rushed down and separated them from their weapons.

The mages hung back at this point, not wanting to waste any of their magical energy. Not that the bad guys had a chance, seeing as how the light had blinded them. That thought set me off singing "Blinded by the Light" and then I couldn't get the lyrics out of my head. Everyone else on the team gave me glares that said it was now locked in their train of thought as well.

I'm sure it's stuck in yours now, too.

Sorry.

"All tied up, Chief," said Chuck, Griff's partner and life-partner.

The two men looked like polar opposites. Where Griff was middle-aged, well-dressed, of average height and build, and somewhat snobbish, Chuck was younger, tall, lanky, had longer hair, and wore long black trench coats. Plus, Chuck was a vampire and Griff was a mage. Not exactly a common combination. Honestly, I couldn't place the chemistry between the two. They came from totally different worlds. Of course, maybe *that's* where the allure was for both of them.

"I'll put them in stasis," declared Warren as he set about drawing up runes.

When I'd first met Warren, I was expecting him to look like Gandalf or Dumbledore. You can imagine how let down I was to instead find a scrawny dude who looked like a flower child from the seventies. Regardless, I'd found him to be quite capable in the realm of wizardry. Yes, he was slower than a sloth, but that was a common theme for wizards.

"Actually," I said, interrupting him before he could get started, "we may need you to disable runes in the house."

"Good point," he agreed.

Jasmine, the dark-haired beauty, who was one of my three mages, stepped up and set her hands to glowing. While all the mages, including Griff, wore leathers as their standard garb, Jasmine had gone with a black ensemble this evening. With the glow of her hands radiating against her pale, white skin, the image was mesmerizing.

Everyone stepped back so as to avoid being caught in whatever web it was that she was unleashing. Everyone except for Felicia, that is. Felicia was Jasmine's partner. Not life-partner. They were both into dudes...though there was mention of Jasmine and Rachel hooking up at one point during a stakeout.

I warmed at the thought.

Felicia had a set of gorgeous brown eyes that were nestled perfectly in her dark-skinned face. She and I had quite a history together, back when I was still allowed to play with the crew. Felicia was seriously hot, but when she started moving into werewolf mode, she got even more smokin'. Her eyes would go from brown to red. Now, when she was fully wolf...well, no. But when she was still human but starting to turn...well, yeah.

A stream of light jettisoned from Jasmine's fingertips and struck skull after skull of the bad guys. They all flopped forward, knocked out.

"They'll be asleep for at least an hour," Jasmine said, looking as though the energy required to cast the spell was minimal. "I didn't want to overdo it."

"Good thinking," I replied. Then I called back to base. "Lydia, could you send Harvey and a pick-up crew to arrest some folks down here?"

Harvey was new to the team. He was part of the invasion force set up by Shitfaced Fred. But Harvey had only participated because his wife, Matilda, was helping Fred at the time, and Harvey was admittedly a bit whipped. That all changed for Harvey, though, and since he'd made a turnaround to help us fight against Fred, he was pardoned of his transgressions. His wife was slated to pay for her crimes by serving a few years in the pen. Anyway, due to Harvey's friendship with Portman, and the way he'd spun himself around to the right side of the law, I ended up getting him a job on our security team. He was now tasked with loading up the guys we arrested in the paddy wagon and bringing them back to the cells.

"You got it, sugar. Do you need Mr. Portman, too?"

Portman was the man in charge at the supernatural morgue in town. He was a werebear. Strong, fast, loyal, and just an all-around good guy. He was also good friends with Harvey, which played in to my giving Harvey the job with pick-up.

"Probably not a bad idea," I stated, thinking that those on the inside had to have been aware of the goings on out here by now. That meant there was a fight coming, which meant bullets would be flying. With me, Chuck, and Felicia all carrying Desert Eagles, that spelled the need for Portman. "Yeah, go ahead and give him the heads-up too, please."

There was a pause. "Do you want me to send in Paula Rose, too?"

Everyone cringed at that thought, especially me.

Paula served as the head of The Spin, an organization whose job it was to put a spin on supernatural events.

Marketing helped keep the locals from going bonkers while also keeping the tourists pouring in. If everyone thought there were a bunch of vampires, werewolves, fae, pixies, djinn, and so on running around the town, there'd be mass panic.

Those creatures, and more, *were* running all over the world, of course. They came up through the Netherworld, which some called the "Labyrinth" due to the odd layout of the place. The Netherworld was accessible via a dimensional portal, of which there were only a few in each city. The majority of supernaturals were allowed to live among the normals as long as they went back every so often for reintegration. It was usually on a thirty-day cycle, but that was extended as the supernatural demonstrated their ability to function nicely in the world of the normals. Everyone went through a psych eval, mental programming to help avoid attacks on normals, and training on the latest techniques to help keep them from getting into trouble.

Anyway, it was Paula's job to keep the normals oblivious as best as possible.

Some normals knew, of course. You couldn't keep something like that from everyone. It just wasn't logistically possible. But those who knew were sworn to secrecy, and if they ended up blabbing, they'd be discredited and made to look the fool.

Worse, Paula was one of my ex-girlfriends. Let's just say that it hadn't ended well.

"I suppose you should," I said with much effort, recalling how Paula had nearly skinned me alive for telling her about the zombie thing a little late. "But tell her not to come down here just yet. I don't want her to make a trip for nothing."

"You got it, lover."

"Ugh," said Rachel, who really despised the fact that Lydia flirted with me.

A window on the second level shattering and the sound of a bullet ricocheting off the ground behind me made it clear that we were in the shit.

"Run," I yelled as everyone scattered toward the house.

If that bullet had been a few inches over, I'd have been pushing up daises. Yeah, I'm strong as an ox and I heal incredibly fast, but a bullet to the skull or the heart would pretty much spell the end of days for me.

"You're lucky that didn't hit me, you fucker," I yelled out.

"Come get some, cop," a gruff voice replied. "Next one won't miss."

I looked across the way and saw two glowing red orbs.

Felicia was pissed.

CHAPTER 4

y first thought was to send a direct message to Felicia, telling her to keep her cool, but then another round of bullets littered the ground in front of us.

"Sic'em," I said to her as if she were a Doberman Pinscher.

Rachel slapped me on the back of my head, but Felicia didn't seem to mind as she howled and then dived through the nearest window.

Soon after, Jasmine blew out the front door with a fireball, clearly wanting to get to her partner as soon as possible. Felicia wasn't bulletproof, after all, and she also wasn't exactly in the proper frame of mind to remember that fact, so we had to cover her back.

I shouldn't have worried.

Felicia was in full wolf form now, meaning her clothes were torn to shreds and she was big and hairy with a long muzzle. This look wasn't exactly what I'd call attractive. Deadly, yes, but not attractive.

Two vampires were lying on the ground, shredded.

There was nobody else around.

Felicia wasn't done, though. She was sniffing the air, trying to catch the scent of her next victim.

"Felicia," I yelled, "heel!"

Rachel slapped me again and this time Felicia gave me a "Do you want to rethink what you just said?" look.

"Sorry," I stated quickly. "I was just…" I trailed off and cleared my throat. "Anyway, I don't want you inadvertently attacking the normal."

"I won't." Her voice was deeper and came out in a growl.

"I'm sure you think that, but there—"

"I won't," she repeated with menace.

"Right."

She looked up the stairs near the end of the room. "I'm going."

"No," I commanded, knowing I had to keep control of the situation. "I can't have you going berserk. It's too risky."

"I said—"

"And I said it's not happening." Our eyes met. Hers were red. Mine were watering. "Now get back into human form while we take care of finding the lady."

She growled, but I held my stare until she tore her eyes away. Dealing with werewolves was rarely fun. Fortunately, Felicia was able to keep her senses about her enough to honor the chain of command.

"Griff and Chuck," I said, quickly changing the point of discussion, "secure the upstairs."

They ran off.

"Jasmine, stay here with Felicia and make sure nobody gets out."

"You got it, Chief," Jasmine replied as she patted Felicia's fur, clearly working to calm her partner down.

"Warren," I said, turning to the wizard, "I have a feeling we're going to find this normal—"

"Her name is Charlotte Davenport," Rachel interjected.

"Swell," I said, noting in my tone of voice that I honestly didn't care at the moment. "Anyway, she's most likely in the basement."

"Why?" said Warren.

"Because that's how these things are done," I explained. "Just watch any movie where there's a kidnapping or a hostage situation and you'll find that they're almost always in the basement."

"Not if it's a bank robbery," Warren pointed out.

"Is this a bank robbery?" I asked pointedly.

"There's another flaw with that theory," Rachel said as Warren studied his feet. "There's no basement in this building."

I went to reply, but she was right. Damn it.

A quick look around the room told me I was in an art gallery of some sort. I was not much in the way of art collecting, but a mostly empty space with paintings hanging on the walls with little lights above them told me all I needed to know.

"Then what's that door lead to?" I asked.

They both looked at me dully.

I reached out.

"You sure you want to do that?" Warren said. "Could be a rune on that door."

"Could you check?" I asked with frustrated sarcasm.

"You got it, Chief," he said, "but it'll take time to figure them out."

Rachel grunted at Warren. "I'll search for the runes and you disable any we find."

This worked out perfectly since Rachel could cast spells fast. She'd be able to highlight any runes in the area much more quickly than Warren could. He'd still have to disable them, but at least it wouldn't take twice as long.

She motioned about with her hands for a few seconds

and then launched a spell at the door, sending down cascades of light like snow flurries.

"Nothing."

"Good," I said, reaching out and pushing the door open.

It was dark inside, but my eyes adjusted almost immediately. It was just a closet. There were boxes stacked up, shelves with various painting supplies, a mop and a broom, and…

I peered down and saw a thin crack of light coming from the back of the space.

Rachel went for the light switch, but I caught her hand and lowered it until she was pointing at the crack of light I'd seen.

"Huh," she said.

I flipped over to my connector so that we could communicate without being heard.

"Obviously there's something in there," I more thought than said, but it was effectively the same thing via the connector. "Check for runes, please?"

Rachel did. Again, there were none.

This made sense seeing that we were standing in a building that was owned or rented by a normal. But the supers who were holding her hostage may have had some skills with runes, or maybe they even had a wizard of their own.

"I'm going through. Cover me."

Pulling forth Boomy, I got set, took a deep breath, and shoved through the door.

CHAPTER 5

*I*t opened up into the kitchen.

"Good find, Ian," Rachel said in snarky way. "If we ever run into another great flour caper, you'll be the guy to call."

I rolled my eyes.

"There was a great flour caper?" asked Warren.

Both Rachel and I stared at him for a moment, regarding his intellect. Well, at least I was doing that. I could only assume Rachel was, too. All I knew was that Rachel wasn't actively judging *my* smarts, or lack thereof, and that was good enough for me.

"Mmm!"

I spun to find a woman tied to a chair. She was in the shadows by a small table.

Next to her stood two very rough-looking fellows.

"Drop 'em," the guy with a beard said.

"What are we dropping, again?" I asked, feeling somewhat concerned.

"Your gun, idiot," Rachel answered for the man, demonstrating that she was again judging my intellect.

"Oh, right."

I lowered my gun to the floor.

"Kick it over."

I did.

Mr. Beard snapped up Boomy. This made me rather uncomfortable. I didn't like it when other people handled my weapon.

"It's gonna be fun shootin' you three," Mr. Beard said as he set his gun down and took aim with mine.

Unfortunately for him, Jasmine and Felicia had walked in from the other side of the kitchen, startling the guy.

I dived forward into a roll as he unleashed a .50 caliber round. It sailed over me as I placed my feet on the underside of the table and kicked it straight up. Ms. Davenport was far enough out of the way that the table didn't impact her, but Mr. Beard and his counterpart, a weathered-looking old guy, took the brunt of the hit dead on.

Mr. Beard fired Boomy again, but this time he only sufficed in knocking a hole in the ceiling.

Rachel and Jasmine launched a line of fireballs at the two men as they screamed and hit the ground, causing Boomy to bounce around on the marble tiles. I'd yanked out my smaller gun and unloaded it through the table.

Everything went silent except for the sobbing cries of Ms. Davenport.

I shoved the table out of the way, picked up Boomy, and pointed it at Mr. Beard.

It was too late. His eyes were lifeless. So were his buddy's. Not only had the fireballs spelled doom, my breaker bullets hit both of them solidly.

"Griff?" I said through the connector. "Chuck? You guys okay?"

"All clear up here, Chief," Chuck replied. "How are things there? We heard noises."

"We're good. Come on back down."

By now, Jasmine had gotten over to the captive normal and set about untying her.

Ms. Davenport was quite the looker. Crimson hair, green eyes, high cheekbones, and she was dressed just like you'd expect an art gallery owner in Las Vegas to dress—to the nines.

"Oh, I don't know how to thank you," she said as Jasmine worked on freeing her hands. "You have no idea how terrified I was! I thought those men were going to kill me!"

"Think nothing of it," I said as I moved back toward Rachel and Warren, always feeling uncomfortable with these praise situations. "We're just doing our jobs."

Ms. Davenport looked like someone who had a serious need for a hug at that moment. She was clearly in a state of shock as the tears streamed down her cheeks.

Once Jasmine finished untying her legs, Ms. Davenport rushed from the chair and came directly toward me.

What was I to do? I had this effect on the ladies in general, but when I was coming in as the knight in shining armor, I was downright irresistible.

"Okay, okay," I said, opening my arms in anticipation.

She pushed past me and buried her head in Warren's chest, hugging him with all her might.

"You saved me," she said as the wizard's face registered the same level of shock that I was currently feeling.

"What the fuck?" I said to nobody in particular.

Rachel, Jasmine, and Felicia all found this rather amusing. They made this abundantly clear by chuckling. Rachel walked over to join the other two ladies on my squad.

"Laugh it up, assholes," I said to them with a frown. "Not cool."

"What's going on?" Chuck asked as he and Griff entered

the room, looking over at Warren and Ms. Davenport, who were still engaged in an embrace.

"Ian thought he was *all that*," Rachel said, still smiling from ear to ear. "Turns out that our art dealer is not attracted to him in the least."

I balked. "She never said that!"

"Artistic liberty," Rachel countered. "We *are* in a studio, after all."

Warren was standing there like a deer in the headlights. He was staring at me apologetically, too. Not that it was his fault or anything, but I appreciated the sentiment.

"Knock, knock," came the booming voice of Portman from the main room. "Any bodies we gotta pick up or are you still in the process of killin' people?"

"In here," called Chuck.

Portman and Harvey stepped around the corner a couple of seconds later. They looked similar to each other, almost as if they could have been brothers. Tall, bulky, hairy. It was a standard werebear thing.

"Looks like Warren's got himself a girlfriend, eh?" said Portman.

"She just needed someone to hug," answered Rachel, "and she found Ian repulsive."

"What?"

"Ah," Portman said, nodding at Harvey. "Told ya, man. Some women just prefer that scrawny-guy look."

Harvey handed over a twenty. Why they were betting on something like that was beyond me. I knew they played poker together and they also hit the casinos a lot, but resorting to betting on something so menial as what women —in general—liked or didn't, teetered on the edge of gambling addiction.

"Or the not-Ian-Dex look," Rachel noted.

I winced at her. "Seriously?"

She glanced away as her smile quickly faded. It was clear that even she realized she'd overstepped a boundary with that remark. Ribbing was fine, but being downright mean about it wasn't really Rachel's thing...typically.

"Thank you for saving me," Ms. Davenport said, looking longingly up into Warren's eyes.

"He flashed a light," I complained. "That's it! I nearly got shot...twice!"

She ignored me and just kept holding Warren as if being in his arms would ward off even the nastiest monster.

Everyone else just giggled.

CHAPTER 6

After Harvey and Portman split with the bad guys and the dead guys, I sent everyone else back to the office so Rachel and I could speak with Ms. Davenport to get the full story. Much to my chagrin, she insisted that Warren stay behind.

We went to a lounge area that had a couple of red fabric chairs and a floral loveseat. Ms. Davenport and Warren took the loveseat.

"So what exactly happened, Ms. Davenport?" I asked, trying to ignore the way she was ogling the PPD's wizard.

She closed her eyes as if gathering herself together.

"They were outside chanting things at the gallery," she said, gripping Warren tightly. "It was like they were placing a curse on my place of business. I was so terrified."

This wasn't going to be easy.

"You're safe now, Ms. Davenport," I said in a steady voice.

"That's right," agreed Warren. "I won't let anything happen to you."

Unable to stop myself, I said, "And as long as the only things that attack us are a bunch of skeletons, he'll be the protector you've always dreamed about. Until then, we need some answers."

"Dick," said Rachel with a cough.

I ignored her.

"What I need to know is if you knew who those people were, Ms. Davenport." She was looking off into nowhere. "Ms. Davenport? Did you know who those men were?"

"Yes," she said distantly. "Before I was an art dealer, I worked as a parole officer."

"For the supernatural community?" asked Rachel, leaning forward.

Ms. Davenport shook her head in confusion.

"What?"

"Never mind," I answered smoothly. "You were saying that you were a parole officer, right?"

"Yes."

"And?"

"I did the job to the letter," she said, just above a whisper. "The two men you killed in the kitchen were out on parole a number of years ago, but they failed to show up as scheduled on multiple occasions. I warned them repeatedly, but they wouldn't listen." She was visibly shaken. "The last time they didn't show, I reported them. They were taken into custody and they swore they'd get me for ratting them out."

She began sobbing on Warren's jacket. He was rubbing her head and saying "There, there" a lot.

I pressed on. "How long ago were you a parole officer, Ms. Davenport?"

Rachel gave me a look that conveyed I should show a little compassion. I don't know how trying to figure out a way to further protect this woman wasn't a sign of compassion, but maybe I was reading things wrong.

"There, there," I said without inflection while staring at Rachel.

She face-palmed in response.

"I quit the very day they threatened me," Ms. Davenport answered finally. "That was three years ago."

"Were there any others or was it just the two men that we ended in your kitchen?"

"Just them," she answered without looking at me. "I assume the rest of the people they'd brought were friends or something. I didn't know any of them."

So this was pretty cut and dried, then. Revenge case. I'd seen them pretty often.

They usually happened when someone revealed the whereabouts of a supernatural who was past due on a reintegration cycle. Newbies in the Overworld—the land of the normals—were held on a tight leash of thirty days per cycle. This meant they could live up with the normals for thirty days, but then had to go back to the Netherworld. It only took an hour or two to complete, but some folks considered it stupid or pointless, and so they refused. The result of that decision was a couple of Retrievers— Netherworld PPD officers who retrieved people who didn't report in—knocking at your door. If you went nicely, they'd slap your wrist and be done with it. If not, you'd end up in prison and have to go through multiple reintegration cycles until they felt you were ready for release. Then, if you wanted to come back to the Overworld, you faced even more cycles. When a person ran from the system, the chances of someone turning them in was high. This was because it'd score that person points with the Netherworld council, and it was *always* wise to be in favor with the council. More often than not, the name of the squealer was learned and the imprisoned party went out of their way to pay that person back. We sometimes saw Retrievers on our route. Local PPD officers and Retrievers weren't exactly known for getting along. Jurisdictional debates and all that got in the way. I never really cared about things of that nature. If they had a perp who was on the run, I let them handle it. If I had a perp on the run and they wanted to get involved, great. As long as the job got done, why should I care who did it?

Regardless, this was a different matter altogether. Ms. Davenport was a normal who was acting as a parole officer. This meant that the guys we'd just killed were being imprisoned in the jail system set up for normals. That wasn't uncommon, and the Netherworld cops allowed it as long as the criminals were kept in cells alone and were allowed back to the Netherworld for proper reintegration. There was no sense in a vampire going nuts in a prison and chomping into a bunch of other inmates, after all.

"So, you had no idea what these men were?" I asked, trying to be delicate.

"If you mean the teeth and…" She paused as a tear ran down her horrified face. "*What* were they?"

"Vampires," answered Warren.

"That's what I thought," Ms. Davenport whispered. "I'd heard rumors, but…" She trailed off.

I stood up. "Right, well, as long as there are no others that you're aware of, Ms. Davenport, I'd say you have nothing left to worry about."

Rachel stood, too.

Warren did not.

"You guys go ahead," he said. "I'll stay here with her for a while. You know, just to make sure she's okay."

The look on his face was sincere, but I couldn't help but think that he may have had other thoughts running through his mind.

"He's not you, Ian," Rachel said, taking me by the hand and pulling me toward the door. "We'll see you tomorrow, Warren. Good night, Ms. Davenport."

When we got out of the house, I shook away from Rachel's kung-fu grip.

"I can find my own way, thank you very much."

"You're acting like a child," Rachel said, spinning on me. "Just because that woman finds Warren more her speed than you, you turn into a huge dick."

"But it's *Warren*," I whined as she strode off to her car. "I mean seriously…Warren!"

CHAPTER 7

*E*ven though the hostage situation was relatively minor in comparison to the ubernaturals event with the Chippendale's-looking mage Reese and the zombie invasion of Shitfaced Fred, the Directors were keen on being updated on everything these days. It was like they were on edge...more than usual.

Thus, I sat before the panel. It was kind of like being before a senate hearing, except that I couldn't see the senators. Well, I *could* now and then, but as soon as I caught a glimpse of them, the memory would fade. This meant I couldn't tell you what any of them looked like.

There were four Directors overseeing my precinct. Silver was the head of the Vegas Vampire Coalition, Zack was the leader of the Vegas Werewolf Pack, O managed the Vegas chapter of the Crimson Focus Mages, and EQK sat at the top of the Vegas Pixies.

"There's really not much to report," I said after pleasantries were exchanged. "An ex-parole-officer-turned-art-dealer pissed off some criminals who had violated parole. They got out of prison and were bent on exacting revenge."

"Then why didn't they?" said Silver.

I blinked at the general location of where he sat.

It was actually a very good point. If the bad guys wanted to kill Ms. Davenport, they could have easily done so. There was no need for sentries or.... I frowned. Yeah, what was it with the sentries?

"That's a really good question, sir."

"I agree," said O. "If these men were intent on killing this ex-parole officer, they would have done so."

"Sounds like what Silver just said," EQK stated.

"You know what I don't understand?" asked Zack.

"Basic math?" answered EQK, even though the question was clearly rhetorical.

To Zack's credit, he pressed on without responding to the pixie's obvious insult.

"Why the sentries?"

I nodded. "I was just thinking the exact same thing, sir. I honestly hadn't even thought of this when we were in the middle of the rescue. Saving the normal was paramount. But now I'm just as baffled as the rest of you."

"I'm not baffled," said EQK. "It's obvious what they were planning to do. Just watch some of your own TV shows, you goddamn idiots."

"Language, EQK," O said in an admonishing tone.

"Fuck you, spellboy."

"Excuse me?"

"You're excused," EQK snapped back before continuing with, "If you morons used your brains at all, you'd see that those dudes were planning on having a little 'fun' with that chick before killing her."

Silence followed that statement.

Truth was, disturbing or not, the pixie was probably correct. If you think about it, these were a couple of guys who were stuck in prison for a few extra years due to Ms.

Davenport turning them in. Female company was not all that available in the prison system, which probably gave them a lot of time to think about all the naughty things they would do to their ex-parole officer before ending her.

"So you think the sentries were put there to make sure nobody interrupted their nefarious plans?" asked Zack.

"If I had a treat, I'd throw you one," EQK answered.

"That's it," said O with a grunt. "EQK, if you can't treat your fellow Directors with a level of respect that is worthy of their positions, we will vote that you are either removed from this council or force you to undergo sensitivity training." He paused. "Are we clear?"

"I thought I *was* treating you guys with a level of respect that is worthy of your positions," EQK replied. "No reason to be a dick fume, Osshole."

Zack was growling lightly, Silver sounded to be giggling, and O was dead silent.

Until...

"Did you just call me Osshole?"

"Oh, come on," EQK replied in exasperation. "Don't tell me you're offended by that, too!"

"How could I not be offended by that? How would you like it if I called you PQK instead of EQK?"

"I don't get it," replied the pixie. "What's it mean?"

"Huh?"

"Well, when I called you Osshole, it's clearly a play on the word asshole. But you changing the E to a P in my name..." He trailed off for a second. "I don't get it."

"There's nothing to get," O replied a moment later. "It's just rude and should bother you."

"Oh, right." EQK cleared his throat. "Yeah, being called PQK is *pretty* upsetting, but if you feel that you must call me that in order to embrace your cultural norms, much like my calling you Osshole allows me to embrace mine, then I shall learn to accept your new name for me…Osshole."

It was becoming more and more obvious that Silver was having as much trouble keeping it together as I was. Zack, ever the diplomat, was not giggling. He was likely more offended at this exchange than O was, but he also knew that if he spoke out, EQK would just give him some name as well.

"I'm glad you're enjoying this, Silver," said O.

"Quite."

"Anyway, sirs," I interrupted before they could go down yet another rabbit hole, "I think that EQK's assessment is pretty logical. As for the sentries, I can only assume they were there to make sure the ex-cons had time in the event that the cops did arrive." It didn't make a ton of sense to me, to be honest, but I couldn't think of any other reason for them to be there. "I suppose we could always question them to see if they'll spill the beans."

"Probably wise," O stated, though there was still an edge to his voice.

I stood up to leave, but Zack asked me to sit back down for a moment.

"There are a couple of points for your department that we need to discuss before you go," he said. "First is that you've been the chief of this division for about five years now. That means it's about time for you to start doing reviews."

I never understood why reviews were done at the five-year mark instead of annually like other places, but I'd guessed it had something to do with how long supernaturals lived.

Honestly, I wasn't looking forward to doing the reviews at all. They would require that I take each of my officers on as a working partner for a week so I could watch them perform their duties firsthand. Since most of them had been in the force longer than me—some lifetimes longer, I felt silly judging them.

"You'll have this entire year to manage it," Zack continued, "so there is no rush."

I sighed and nodded.

"Secondly, please remember that it's your duty to make sure your team members adhere to the reintegration rules. We don't want another incident with the Retrievers."

I couldn't argue with him on that point. During my third month as chief, our tech guy, a pixie by the name of Turbo, had forgotten to go back to the Netherworld for reintegration. They sent up an officer to retrieve him, and she gave *me* quite an earful. Apparently, since I was the chief, *I* was on the hook as the first line of making my crew go in for reintegration if they were delayed. The thinking was that I could allow that delay if the officer was in the middle of a case, but I had to notify the Retrievers about it so that they'd hold off on their duties. But Turbo hadn't been doing anything besides his normal day-to-day job, so he should have gone. Apparently the Directors all had to go through additional training because of my slip up, so I couldn't blame them for wanting me to stay on top of things, but they didn't have to remind me every three months.

"I got it, sir," I said evenly. "You may recall that I've not had a single officer skip that duty in roughly five years now."

"Just making sure it stays that way," replied Zack. "Dismissed."

CHAPTER 8

$\mathcal{I}$ called everyone to the conference room to discuss reviews and such. This was my first time having to do this, since the previous chief handled the last round, but it was my duty now.

"Listen up, gang," I said, calming the chatter. "I just got out of a meeting with the Directors and it seems as though five-year reviews are due this year."

There were "ughs" and grumbles all around, except for Harvey. He just looked confused at why review-time was a bad thing. I remembered feeling that way when I'd first started on the force, too. Fortunately for me, the chief had finished up his reviews a couple of weeks before he'd retired his post.

"I know, I know," I said, holding up my hands. "You've all told me that you don't like going through these things. Honestly, I've never been through one as a chief before. I was only here a couple of years before I inherited the chief's duties, and the Directors handled mine by simply saying I was doing a fine job." I rubbed my eyes. "Well, EQK said something a bit more derisive, but it meant about the same thing in his way of speaking."

Their faces were all blank. Again, except for Harvey.

What I *should* have done was bring each of them to those meetings during their review week. That would teach them to show me a little more respect. Either that, or they'd "inadvertently" send a stray fireball my way now and then during a battle.

"Right. Well, I'll probably start things up in a couple of weeks. I need time to get everything straightened out first and do a little research with Lydia so I know what I'm doing. I promise to make things as painless as possible."

Harvey's hand went up.

"Yes, Harvey?"

"I've only been on the job for a little while, boss," he said, sounding more excited than he should have, "but I wouldn't mind going on one of these weeks with you, if that's okay?" He glanced around the room. "I know I'm not really a cop, but I'd like to learn."

It was nice to see at least one member of my team showing some enthusiasm.

I gave that enthusiasm about three months.

"We'll see how things go, Harvey," I said with a nod. "Just keep doing your job for now, okay?"

He pointed at me and winked. "You got it, boss."

"Right, well, only other business I've got is that Serena is due for a reintegration visit to the Netherworld."

She moaned.

It wasn't the kind of moan she used to make back in the day, either. This one was more of the irritated type. Hearing it resulted in a bit of stirring in my lower section, though, because Serena and I used to engage in role playing. She played the part of succubus and I was the lucky bastard serving her.

I shivered slightly.

"It only takes a couple of hours," I soothed, "and you'll be clear for another few months."

"Yes, I know," she replied in a defeated tone of voice. "I'll take care of it this weekend."

"Thank you." I closed up my notepad. "Well, if there's nothing else…" Warren's hand went up. He seemed more chipper and engaged than usual. I could only imagine that Ms. Davenport had something to do with that. "Yes, Warren?"

"I was wondering if you would all be up for joining me and Charlotte tonight for a get-together," he said.

All faces turned toward him.

"That was fast," said Rachel, smiling genuinely. "You guys really hit it off, eh?"

"She's great," Warren said, beaming. "I showed her my runes—"

"They're called balls, pal," I said with a scoff. "Just because you're a wizard doesn't mean you should call your junk after wizarding names."

"I'm talking about my drawings, Chief."

Rachel shook her head at me, clearly disappointed. At least she didn't call me an idiot, aloud anyway.

"Just ignore him, Warren," Felicia said. "He's just jealous."

"I am not."

"What did Ms. Davenport have to say about your drawings, Warren?" asked Griff.

"She wants to do a show for them at her gallery."

The entire team was full of smiles at this. What the hell? They were just pictures of goofy shapes and such. What was the big deal?

"That's great, Warren," Chuck said, slapping the smaller man on the shoulder. "Good for you, man."

"Thanks. Anyway, if you guys would join us for a drink, that would be great."

They were all nodding except for me, but Warren looked up at me with his puppy dog eyes, so I said, "Nope. Definitely not. I have a thing with a chick at the place and I—"

"He'll be there," Rachel stated while giving me a stern look.

"Great!"

Everyone stood up and walked out of the room, leaving me alone with my thoughts.

"That wasn't very nice, sugar plum," said Lydia a few moments later. "You know Warren looks up to you."

If Lydia was giving me crap about this, then I was clearly in the wrong. She sided with me about everything.

"He does?"

"Everyone does, sweet cheeks. That's all part of being the chief."

I had the feeling Lydia was getting her information from old novels and TV shows. Still, it *was* my duty to be supportive of my crew. Usually this meant as far as their jobs went, but even I had to admit that I was being a bit of a tool at the moment.

"Jealousy doesn't become you, lover," Lydia added. "You're better than that."

"You're right, Lydia. Thanks, baby."

"Anytime, honey buns."

*a*n hour later we were sitting at Piero's. I wasn't very hungry, but I could down a plate of pasta and have a drink or two.

Warren and Charlotte didn't exactly look like a match made in heaven. She was gorgeous, and he was...well, Warren. But she *did* appear to genuinely like him, and that softened me a bit. It made me realize that everyone was right: I was being an ass.

And so I lifted my glass and said, "To Warren and Charlotte, may this be the beginning of a long-lasting relationship."

"Cheers to that!" Warren said and everyone laughed.

Rachel gave me a wan smile.

She leaned over. "Just when I think you're incorrigible, you do something like that."

"Oh, don't worry," I replied, holding up my drink, "I'll screw it up eventually."

"I have no doubt," she replied. "But for now, it's nice."

"Gee, thanks."

The pasta was actually pretty tasty and my appetite was

coming back. This probably had a lot to do with the Rusty Nail I was currently downing, but I'm sure that getting over myself, as Rachel put it, was also helpful.

Why should I be irritated about the fact that some chick preferred Warren's company over mine?

But that wasn't the point, was it? No! The fact was that he flashed a stupid light and then just stood around while I got shot at twice before taking down both of the men who were bent on doing nefarious things to Ms. Davenport. Didn't that warrant me at least a "Thank you"?

I grumbled again and looked down at my plate.

Just as I was shoveling in another forkful of yumminess, Charlotte tapped her wine glass with the smooth side of a spoon.

I glanced up to see that Turbo, our little pixie who wore a full officer's uniform, badge and all, was standing on her shoulder.

"Excuse me, everyone," she said, lowering our table's chatter. "I'm sorry to interrupt, but I wanted to share something with you that..." She paused and looked over at Warren. "Actually, did you want to tell them?"

"No, it's okay. Go ahead."

"You sure?"

He nodded, his face lighting up like a beacon.

"Well, I was so impressed with the artwork that Warren does that I've set up something special." She put her hand on his arm. "Technically, *we* set it up, but you know what I mean."

"You guys literally just met last night," I said with a laugh. "How did you have time to set anything up?"

"I already had a bunch of runes drawn up, Chief," explained Warren. "They've been piling up in my guest room for years."

"Exactly," said Charlotte. "Well, he brought me over this

afternoon and showed me his work." She brought her hand to her chest dramatically. "I was so taken aback with the beauty of Warren's art that I felt it just *needed* to be shown to the world."

The entire crew seemed very supportive of this, based on their smiles and nods, but I saw a problem that they were obviously missing. These were runes we were talking about here. They weren't just some random pieces of art.

I knew I was going to take some instant flack, but it was my duty to say something.

"Sorry," I said, leaning forward, "but couldn't it be a bad thing to show your runes to the public?"

I hadn't considered it before, and clearly neither had anyone else. My guess was that they were all enthralled with Warren's newfound love, and I was immersed in a vat of ignorance.

As if commonsense had returned, all their shoulders slumped. Everyone but Charlotte Davenport's, anyway.

"I don't understand," she said. "What's the problem?"

"Runes aren't just pieces of art," Warren replied, looking instantly bummed out. "They can be used for supernatural purposes."

"Even better," Charlotte exclaimed. "People will flock to see that. They *love* magic!"

I cleared my throat and motioned for Warren to explain why this was a bad thing. It was bad enough that I was the one bringing it to everybody's attention, I wasn't going to push myself further into the bad-guy corner.

"We can't risk normals getting their hands on these designs. They're intricate and more complex than people may think, and they take *a lot* of concentration to draw properly, but in the wrong hands they could be really bad."

"Oh?" Charlotte looked confused. "I had no idea."

So much for that plan.

I felt like a heel, but it just wasn't worth the risk.

"I have a solution," said Rachel. "Draw up some others that are just as nice but that have zero magical capability at all."

Charlotte's eyes lit up again.

"Can you do that?" she asked Warren.

"Sure, I guess." He looked unsure. "I've honestly never tried, but I can't see why I couldn't."

"That would be perfect."

Charlotte was nearly giddy. It was rather unnerving. I got it, that being pulled out of a dangerous situation by someone —even if it wasn't the someone who *actually* saved you— could cause a solid emotional response, but this was over the top.

Still, Warren was happy and that meant I was happy. According to Rachel and Lydia, anyway.

"Well," Charlotte said a moment later, "could we still show *them* what we did this afternoon?" She was smiling at Warren like a kid in a candy store. "We'll replace the pieces before showing the general public, of course."

He licked his lips. "I guess that'd be okay. Right, Chief?"

"I haven't the foggiest idea what you're talking about," I answered, "but as long as only those of us at this table are the ones seeing your work, it should be fine. Unless any of the mages here disagree?"

Griff, Jasmine, and Rachel looked back and forth at each other.

"Should be okay," said Jasmine.

"I see no issues with it," agreed Griff.

Rachel nodded and held up her glass. "It's fine."

Perfect. Now none of them could blame me if things *did* go horribly wrong. Not that they would. Probably. But if they did, it wouldn't be my fault.

Well, technically, it *would* be my fault seeing that any

failings of any officer ultimately fell on the shoulders of the chief, which in turn got dumped onto the shoulders of the Directors. The Netherworld Council was involved above that, but I rarely let my mind drift that far into the realm of the political world. I found the life of chasing naughty monsters far safer than inserting myself into the folly of debating politics.

"I think it's a wonderful idea," chimed in Turbo. "Just wonderful!"

"Excellent," exclaimed Charlotte, clapping her hands. "Let's go, then."

"Where are we going again?" I asked, lowering my fork.

"Back to my art gallery," she answered while grabbing Warren by the arm and pulling him along.

Turbo said, "Weeeeee" as they sped out of the restaurant.

CHAPTER 10

The art gallery was slightly different as we walked in. There were still paintings hanging on the walls, but they weren't the same ones as before. There were now a smattering of intricate drawings that clearly came from the hand of Warren.

Again, I'm no art collector, but these were some pretty stunning runes. I'd seen the basic ones he'd drawn many times over the years, and I'd even seen a few that were rather detailed, but these were incredible. The lines and shapes were masterfully crafted, but it was the interwoven patterns, colors, and shading that nearly made my eyes pop out.

"Wow," I said while putting a hand on Warren's shoulder. "These are amazing, Warren."

"You really think so?"

"I know so."

I honestly had to spend more time getting to know each of my officers. It was easy to take their skills for granted, but seeing this level of talent only made me wonder what the rest of my crew were capable of...beyond unleashing hell in the face of adversity, of course.

"Honestly, I'm floored."

"Thanks, Chief. That means a lot."

We all milled about for a few minutes as we studied each painting. It was deathly silent, which meant I wasn't the only one who was dumbfounded by Warren's mad skills.

"Excuse me, everyone," Charlotte said, jolting me from nearly falling in love with a rune painting entitled "Reverie." I had no idea what it actually did—it *was* a rune, after all, but I was damn sure going to have to buy it. "If you'll all come over here and stand in this section, there is a special surprise that we have for you."

We walked over and Charlotte moved us all so that we were kind of squished together.

"Sorry," she said. "I know it's kind of tight, but we'll work that out before the main show." She then turned to Warren. "Of course, if we won't be able to use real runes, then this part of the show wouldn't work anyway, right?"

"That's true."

"Hmmm." Her look of concern morphed back into a grin. "No matter. I think everyone will love it anyway."

"Hard to argue that," I agreed. "Your art is..." I looked around again. "It's fantastic."

Everyone murmured their agreement, including Turbo, which made Charlotte jump.

"Oh! I nearly forgot you were there, little friend." She put her hand out and he hopped on. That was saying something considering that Turbo was usually pretty stern about jumping into people's hands. "If you could join your friends, I think you're really going to love this."

"Okay!"

Turbo buzzed over, passed by my ear, and landed on Harvey's shoulder, who was standing right behind me. He and Harvey had hit it off pretty soon after the werebear joined the force. They were both excitable types. It was kind of cool to see Turbo fly about with his little officer's outfit on. Obviously he'd designed it in such a way that his wings were able to sprout out the back. He was an ingenious little guy.

"Are you all ready?" Charlotte asked as though she were about to sing "Happy Birthday" to a five-year-old. She was clearly enthralled with whatever was about to happen.

"I am," Harvey said with a level of enthusiasm that mimicked Charlotte's. "This is the most fun I've had in ages."

My first thought was to find Harvey's comment difficult to believe. Then I recalled that he'd been subjected to a lot of mental berating from his wife over the years. To him, hanging out with this crew in any context was probably like finding paradise.

Rachel and I shared a smile, seeing that we were both present when Harvey finally grew a set of balls and had stood up to Matilda, his now-imprisoned overbearing wife.

"Great, Harvey," Charlotte said. "Okay, Warren, show them your magic."

Our flower child of a wizard walked over and pulled out another canvas from behind a small covering. It was a rune that had multiple lines connected to a series of smaller runes. I did another inventory of the gallery and realized that it was a miniature depiction of the room we were in.

"This one was Charlotte's idea," Warren said. "It's meant to bring everything together. I think it looks pretty cool, but it's also functional."

"How so?" asked Chuck.

"It's part of the show," Charlotte said, waving at Chuck in a "hush" kind of way while giving him a wink. "You'll see soon enough."

Charlotte motioned Warren to go ahead. Then she stepped back and gave him the stage.

"Okay," he said in a shaky voice. "I'm a little nervous here, so I'm sorry if I screw up."

We all laughed.

"Right."

He cleared his throat and stood up tall. There was a sudden showmanship in his presence.

"Around you is a set of my most magical runes. They have powers beyond what the eye can see."

I was impressed. He was really going all-in with this. Sad that he'd not be able to use actual runes for obvious reasons, though. It would make for one heck of a show.

"And this rune," he continued, waving his hand dramatically over the one he was holding, "is the key to them all. It opens the doorway to a shared imagination."

He began tracing his fingers along the lines, causing each of the smaller runes around the edge to light up as they connected to the center. I glanced around and noticed that the runes on the walls were lighting up as well.

"Cool as shit," I whispered.

"Really is," Rachel said as she grabbed my hand.

My eyes went wide, as did hers.

She let go.

"Your minds will wander. Your souls will seek the far reaches of the universe. Your hearts will soar!"

All runes were glowing now, pulsing in unison. A tingling sensation ran up my body. It wasn't exactly unpleasant, but I could have done without it. I assumed it was just one of the kinks they still had left to work out.

"When I say the magic word," Warren spoke like a magician running a show on the Strip, "your worlds will change."

I had no idea what was coming, but this show could rake in millions if they figured out a way to do it without people really knowing what the runes represented. I had an idea for that, too. Simply put the real runes behind the fake ones. Nobody would be able to see the real ones, but the show could still go on. I'd have to share this with Warren and Charlotte when everything was said and done. Hell, I'd have to invest in this, too. The return would be insane!

"Transfera impactus!"

Everything went dark and the tingling turned into full-on shock.

It was *not* pleasant. In fact it burned like hell. On top of that, my stomach flipped upside down. I felt like I was going to decorate the floor.

Then I heard the sound of retching behind me, and it was followed by a splash on my back.

"What the hell?" I said, groaning angrily at the recognition that another of my suits had been destroyed.

"Sorry, boss," was all Harvey could say.

"Me, too," agreed Turbo.

"Well, thanks a lot," I stated, noting that my nausea had somewhat subsided. "Next time could you maybe turn your heads?"

"Sorry," they both said again, this time in unison.

I couldn't see anything then, which was odd since my eyesight was known to be quite decent in the dark. That meant that this wasn't just a trick of the light. Something was actually going on besides just trickery.

"What's happening anyway?" I asked. "It was fun at the start, but this whole section of the show kinda sucks."

In response to my question, the world faded back into view.

We were no longer in the gallery.

Unless my mind was fooling me, which certainly could have been the case since this was all part of a magic show, of sorts, we were standing in the middle of the Badlands in the Netherworld.

Then I got the sudden impression that this *wasn't* a show, after all.

I came to this conclusion because Charlotte was no longer the happy-go-lucky-looking chick she'd been before. She was now wearing a tight-fitting black leather outfit, dark liner around her eyes, and a heavy scowl on her face.

Next to her stood an elderly wizard who *did* look like Gandalf, except that this guy had glowing blue eyes.

I gulped as I stared down at Warren's limp body. He was facedown in the dirt.

My mind raced as I pulled my gaze back up until I was staring into the eyes of Charlotte Davenport.

"What the fuck's going on?"

CHAPTER 11

*C*harlotte was pacing back and forth in front of us like some kind of prison warden.

We couldn't break free of the space that we were in. This obviously had something to do with the spell that our very own Warren had placed on us.

I stared down at him again.

Who could blame him, though? The fact was that *I* was acting jealous of the guy. It could have been me lying in the dirt...

Actually, no, it couldn't have.

Son of a bitch.

Charlotte had selected Warren specifically for this...well, whatever the hell it was. She didn't bypass me because she thought Warren had saved her or because she found him more attractive than me. She did it because Warren was a goddamned wizard!

"So this was all a setup?" I laughed in a not-so-funny way.

"Obviously, genius," said Rachel in one of her attitude-laced tones. "What I want to know is why?"

"Because I needed him," Charlotte said, pointing at

Warren. "And I knew that if he disappeared, you'd all come hunting for him."

"So you brought us down here to make it easier for us to hunt you down?" I asked while tilting my head to the side. "That's just dumb."

She grinned evilly and stepped up to me.

Chuck and Felicia began going for their weapons.

"Don't," I said through the connector with a warning glance at them. "We don't know if she's aware that we have the guns or not. She probably thinks we were all out on the town, so why bother to bring our weapons?"

They lowered their hands.

"I'm aware that you have your guns, Officer Dex," she said, making me blanch.

"You can hear my thoughts?"

"What?" she asked, frowning. "No. Why would you think that?"

"Uh...because...well...never mind."

"Your movements give you away, I'm afraid," explained Charlotte. "It's in my nature to notice even the smallest things."

"Idiot," Rachel said through the connector.

"Give me a break," I spat back. "It was pretty damn coincidental, wouldn't you say?"

There was no reply, which was as solid as a full-on apology when it came to Rachel.

What did Charlotte mean about noticing minute things?

I studied her more closely, watching the way she moved. She was lithe. Her stride was so smooth it was almost as if she were doing ballet as she walked. Not that there was dancing going on or anything, but the grace was the same. She kept her arms crossed and a sneer on her face, which didn't tell me much other than she could be Rachel's fraternal twin.

The makeup she wore might have signaled her as being a succubus, except for the fact that the black lines that left the corners of her eyes morphed into a crimson color that came to a swirled end. Succubi didn't do that. At least none that I knew, and I knew a lot of them.

Vampire and werewolf were out, too. While vampires were pretty graceful in their own right, this chick went way beyond them. Werewolves were not graceful. They clomped like big-footed St. Bernards.

She could have been a fae. They were notoriously good-looking. Still, though, her movements…

"Who were the two men we killed at your house?" asked Felicia. "They obviously weren't there to take you down or do anything naughty to you."

"You're right about the first part," Charlotte answered. "They were originally there to do something naughty with me, but it was consensual. Then I…coerced them into the second part of my plan."

I blanched. "So I put a bunch of holes in a couple of innocents?"

Charlotte laughed at my outburst.

"I don't know that I'd call them innocents, Officer Dex. They were my servants." She looked at her black, pointy nails. "Don't worry, though. They were expendable."

"Oh, well, that makes me feel better, then."

"Good," she said and then snapped her fingers and pointed at Warren.

The wizard behind her pulled out a wand and flicked it at our wizard. A light surrounded him like a cocoon, lifting him off the ground. Either Gandalf had already had that spell at the ready or he was a lot faster at the wizard game than Warren was.

Our poor wizard had his eyes shut and he looked to be in a fair amount of pain.

"What have you done to him?" I asked, trying to push through the barrier in front of me.

"He's in stasis for now," she answered, obviously finding my concern amusing. "Just last night you were all worried about why I was more interested in him than I was in you, and now you're worried about his wellbeing? Isn't that sweet, Melvin?"

"Yes, my lady," the wizard replied in a squeaky voice that befitted someone of his years.

"So, wait, obviously that entire show of affection to Warren was fake," I said. "Does this mean that you really thought *I* was—"

Rachel slapped me before I could finish.

"What?"

"Seriously, you have to ask that right now, you self-centered, narcissist?" She shook her head at me and then turned back to Charlotte. "Why would you bring us here if you knew we were going to hunt you for kidnapping Warren?"

"Because I had to make sure you were out of the way, Officer Cress," Charlotte replied as Melvin the wizard levitated and sped away with a floating Warren in tow. "With you in my land, I don't have that worry. Plus, it will allow me to exact my full plan on the Vegas Strip without interference from the PPD."

"How does that make any sense at all?" I asked.

"Because, Officer Dex, it'll be impossible for you to chase me if you're no longer alive."

Again, I pushed against the energy field that was imprisoning my crew. It didn't budge.

"You're a mean person," said Turbo out of nowhere. "I thought you were nice, but you're nothing but a stinky bottom."

I looked over my shoulder. "A stinky bottom?"

"What's wrong with that?"

"What *isn't?*" I countered.

"Well, I'm sorry you feel that way, little pixie," Charlotte answered with a faux pout. "All I can say is that pretty soon you won't have to worry about being angry anymore."

"So, what then?" Harvey barked. "Are you just going to kill us in this little pen, you horrible piece of poop?"

I looked back again. "Are you two brothers or something?"

"No, why?"

Charlotte stepped away from the boundary, moving back to the edge of a cliff. She glanced over the side and smiled. The area was orange and glowing brightly.

"I'll let you out of your pen in a moment," she answered finally. "My children couldn't devour you otherwise."

Her children?

That's when it hit me.

"Oh, shit," I said as Charlotte crossed her hands in the shape of an X and then threw them out to her sides. "She's a fucking dragon."

CHAPTER 12

*B*y the time the metamorphosis completed, we were staring up at a dragon that stood a good twenty feet tall.

Her leathery wings flapped as she stared down at us. The size of her muzzle alone could have housed Harvey with room to spare.

And she wasn't nearly as attractive in dragon form either. Frankly, had I known from the start, I wouldn't have complained one bit that she'd selected Warren over me.

I'd gone out with a dragon once, before I was a cop. She was one of the sweet types, but only while I was with her. When we split up, it was a nightmare. Some people get territorial, but dragons take it to an entirely new level. They considered themselves as part of your existence until you either died or were replaced. Fortunately, for me, another dragon happened to have moved into the area and they hit it off.

"Come, my children," called Charlotte. Her voice was booming yet still feminine.

A few moments later, three dragons that were half her size crested the ravine. Two male and one female.

If there was one thing worse than standing under a dragon, it was standing under two. Seeing that there were now four of the beasties flapping away above us, I found myself terrified.

Charlotte dropped something that she'd been holding in her talon. It crashed on the ground, splintering into a number of pieces.

The forcefield around us disintegrated.

I studied the pieces of the item she dropped and recognized that it was the final painting Warren had displayed when he was doing his act.

"You may all run now," Charlotte said. "My children prefer to hunt their meals down."

"Nobody move," I said. "If they want to hunt, then we'll just have to disappoint them."

"They'll still eat you, Officer Dex," Charlotte replied with a chuckle. "It just won't be nearly as fun for them."

"Oh."

"Now, my children," Charlotte said, spinning to face the other three dragons, "once you're done feeding, join me at the tower. I will have need of your assistance once the ritual is complete."

I started scanning the area.

There were caves and hills and jutting rocks all over the place. The only safe haven seemed to be the caves, but seeing that the cave mouths were so large, I doubted it would keep any of the dragons out. Still, they couldn't *all* follow us in. Divide and conquer was a more likely winning scenario than trying to take on all three of them at once.

"Gang," I said through the connector, "when I give the word, run to a cave and get in as far as possible. If we split them up and attack, we may just have a chance."

"We'll throw some magic up to start the attack first," Rachel replied. "That will give the rest of you time to escape."

"Have fun, Officer Dex," Charlotte said before turning to fly away.

Her laughter could be heard until she disappeared behind the shadow of a large mountain. Way off in the distance I spotted a tower on top of a tall mountain. It was ridiculously cliché, but that tended to be how things worked with dragons. I zoomed my sight to find that the wizard was already approaching the place. Whatever magic he was employing was rather powerful indeed.

Once Charlotte was out of eyesight, the three younger dragons spun to face us.

"Run," the one in the center commanded.

"Wait, wait, wait," I said, holding up my hands while giving my mages a moment to prepare themselves. My only hope was that these younger dragons weren't as experienced as their mother. "You really shouldn't eat us."

"Why not?"

"It's not healthy, that's why not."

"What?"

"Study after study has shown that meat can cause all sorts of physical ailments."

The dragons looked at each other. "Like what?"

"Clogged arteries, for one," I answered. "I mean, the studies seem to change every week, but most people still think that red meat is not all that great for you." I shook my head sadly at them. "The last thing you want is to have a heart attack when you're fifty because you weren't careful with your diet at twenty."

The dragons conferred for a moment, giving my crew the time they needed to prepare.

Chuck and Felicia already had their weapons drawn. Harvey was in the process of morphing into a werebear, and

Turbo had taken out a miniature version of Boomy. I had to grin at that. It couldn't have housed anything larger than a .000050 caliber bullet.

The dragons turned back.

"We discussed it," announced the one in the middle. "There's plenty of time for us to eat salads after tonight. For now, we shall indulge ourselves."

"Indulge?" I said with my eyes up. "That's a pretty big word for such a young dragon."

That was obviously the wrong thing to say because her brow creased ferociously.

I turned to my crew and yelled, "Run!"

CHAPTER 13

On the off-chance that you've never been chased by a dragon, it's a lot scarier than you may think.

While these particular dragons weren't likely to blow a sheet of flame at us—seeing that they probably wanted to eat us alive—the realization that they *could* light us up any time they wanted was enough to make me want to mess my shorts. Of course, the realization that they wanted to eat me alive didn't much help matters.

Fortunately, the mages were keeping them somewhat busy with bolts of ice. Flames weren't nearly as effective on dragons as they were on other races. If the dragon was in human form, it worked okay, but still not as well as cold spells.

None of my crew wanted to take off for the caves. I understood that. Members of their team were here fighting, so to leave would feel seriously wrong.

But the team was fighting *so* they could get away.

"Chuck, Serena, Felicia, Harvey, and Turbo," I yelled, "get your asses moving!"

"You too, Ian," Rachel called over her shoulder. "You're no good here."

"Sure, I am," I said, whipping forth Boomy.

I calmed my racing heart, steadied my breath, and pulled the trigger.

The breaker bullet ricocheted off the center dragon's chest and struck the one to its right on a talon.

The beast screeched.

"Ian," Rachel screamed, "get the hell out of here!"

"Nope," I said calmly through the connector as the others were running for the caves. "You three are more important than me. I can't keep the rest of the team alive. You can."

"He's right," said Jasmine. "We're just going to run out of steam out here."

I nodded while aiming at one of the talons on the center dragon. The breaker struck it and it roared, pulling its leg up.

Then it turned on me with rage in its eyes.

"Super," I said, honestly worried I was going to soil myself. "Well, I know how to get their attention now."

A shimmering appeared in front of me as the dragon I'd struck got a look in its eyes that conveyed it was about to burn me to a crisp.

"I just cast a spell of protection on you," Griff stated. "It will only last a couple of minutes, though."

"You can't afford that type of energy drain, Griff," Jasmine countered.

"It had to be done," he said in a labored voice.

"Two minutes should be enough for you to get safely to the caves," I said, pulling up Boomy again and ripping off two more rounds, which smacked the talons on the other two. "Go!"

I took off to the left, heading toward a cave that was about twice the distance away than the one my team had retreated toward. There was no way I was going to make it, but that wasn't my goal anyway. I was simply a diversion.

It was working, too.

A massive ball of flame burned all around me, melting rock and scorching the air.

Griff's protection spell was working wonderfully, but I could still feel the temperature rise. Not drastically, but it was apparent. To be fair, that could have been a psychological reaction due to the fact that my brain believed I *should* be feeling the heat. Mental or not, I was sweating.

I glanced over my shoulder and found that only two of the beasts were after me. The other one was chasing my mages.

Rachel and Jasmine were casting ice spells over their shoulders in haphazard fashion to delay its pace. Again, the dragon wasn't likely going to flame them, and they could ward off the one while retreating. Three? No. But one should be doable.

A talon grabbed my left shoulder and started to dig in.

This told me that the shield Griff cast on me was only effective against fire.

Fantastic.

The pain was immense as the talon pinched tighter and started lifting me off the ground. I pulled out Boomy and fired a round straight into the beast's soft palm, causing it to screech and let go.

I crashed to the ground, slamming my hip on a rock in the process. It wasn't pleasant.

At least I'd kept my hold on Boomy, which was rather surprising considering how hard I'd landed.

"Shit," I yelped, rolling onto my back as the second dragon flew over and unleashed a massive blast of flame directly at me.

The blaze lasted a good twenty seconds, as did the

uncontrollable yell of terror that burst from my lungs. When it finally subsided, I was lying in a mixture of lava and booty oopsie.

Yes, it was quite embarrassing, but how many people can claim to have shit themselves while surviving the full brunt of dragon flame? That's a story you tell your grandkids.

The dragon looked completely shocked to see me stand back up.

"You have a spell on you," it said curiously. "You are shielded from our flame."

"Your mother must be proud," I responded in a very shaky voice. "Your powers of deduction are rather impressive."

I knew it was dumb to further irritate the dragons, but my mages weren't quite safe, yet.

"This one is a waste of our time," the dragon stated, probably thinking I'd meant what I'd said genuinely. You'd think that dragons would get sarcasm better than most. "We must help Sister."

"But he shot our feet!"

"They'll heal," the larger one said sternly. "Let's go."

As they turned, I unloaded Boomy at their legs, but my breathing was very erratic and my aim was terrible.

Damn it!

There was no way I could catch up to them at this point unless I used *Haste*, which would give me a lot of speed, but I didn't think I could control it right now. My body was frazzled and my mind wasn't much better.

And that meant my team was on their own.

The shield that Griff had given me shimmered and disappeared.

"They're coming back, guys," I said through the connector, feeling defeated. "Get in the cave and blow away the rock face to lock yourselves inside. I'm going through the cave on this side. Hopefully they'll connect. One way or the other, I'll get to you. Keep me posted."

"They *do* connect, Ian," Griff said in a tired voice. "It won't be easy, though."

"Never is," I replied. "Don't worry about me. Get yourselves to safety."

"Be careful, Ian," Rachel said in a desperate voice.

She had connected directly to me so that the others couldn't hear her.

I zoomed my vision and saw she was looking at me.

"You too, Rachel." I slammed my eyes shut. "Take care of the others. You're in charge until I get through."

With that, I spun and ran toward the cave.

CHAPTER 14

I felt the connector go dead as soon as I entered the cave mouth.

The device worked via satellites, cell towers, Netherworld towers, and line-of-sight. The Badlands were devoid of the standard tech and the cave blocked direct connection.

Bottom line was that I was cut off from my team in more ways than one.

That wasn't good.

It was bad enough that I was separated from them, but now I didn't even know how they were doing. All I could hope for was that they'd gotten to safety and sealed themselves in. The dragons would remove the rocks through fire or force, but having the barrier would at least delay them getting through.

For now, though, I had to focus on my own situation.

There's a reason why people are told to put their oxygen masks on themselves first during those safety readings before a plane takes off. If you put it on yourself, you'll be able to help others around you because you won't black out.

On the contrary, if you try to help everyone else out first, you'll all black out.

So, I had to take care of myself first.

I put my back against the wall and gave my eyes a couple of seconds to adjust. I didn't need much time. My eyes were special that way.

Even if I weren't an amalgamite, I could have cast a small light spell. Not that I was great in the ways of magic, but I had a few tricks up my sleeve.

There was a tunnel running down deeper into the Netherworld. It wasn't the most enticing thing to go toward, but with my team in trouble, I saw no other option.

Before jumping to it, though, I thought back to everything I'd learned about the Badlands.

There were numerous courses that I was put through before I was allowed to wear a PPD badge. Most of them were in the realm of firearms, hand-to-hand combat, criminal rights, and leadership skills. I even had to take a class on Retriever law. That wasn't much fun. While I didn't commit it to memory, the Retrievers had to recite a legal phrase to the perp upon arresting them. It was kind of like the normals and their Miranda Rights, but stranger.

None of those courses were going to help here, though, except the firearms and hand-to-hand stuff, obviously.

I needed to lean on my knowledge regarding geography and races in the Badlands.

Sadly, I sucked at geography. It was boring.

"When am I ever going to use this?" I said aloud, mocking my younger self. "Idiot."

In my defense, I'd been in my early twenties during that training and had fully planned on working for the PPD in the Overworld. I'd never entertained the possibility of landing in the Badlands. Who would?

So here I was, standing in a cave and looking down a

tunnel that connected to a world unlike the one I was used to. My connector was out, there was no such thing as Google Netherworld that covered this place, and even if there had been, it wasn't like I could get cell reception.

What I *did* have was Boomy and a good number of magazines. I always carried ample amounts of breaker bullets. That was one thing I learned during my many battles as a PPD officer, and I didn't need school to learn that.

"Okay, Ian," I whispered, "we know there are various races down here. Some of them are harmless and will just stick to themselves, but there are others that are quite dangerous."

Three, in fact.

This was something that they drilled into our heads during the Badlands discussions.

"If you learn nothing else in this class," I recalled the teacher saying, "remember that you *do not* want to tangle with demons, dragons, and…"

I blanked.

What the hell was the third one? Obviously it was important because the teacher said it was really important.

Shit.

Well, I'd already dealt with demons before. They weren't a lot of fun. In fact, had it not been for Warren's void wall back when we faced those beasts, I would have been pushing up daisies. That made me wonder where they went when they entered that void wall. If it was down here, I was screwed. In fact, my entire team was screwed. I doubted demons forgot things like that. I wouldn't.

Dating dragons, or a *dragon*, was something I'd done, but fighting them was new. They were purported to be cunning of mind and fierce in battle, but the three juveniles seemed easily fooled to me. The image returned of that one hovering over me and releasing a stream of fire. I shuddered.

That's when I remembered that my shorts weren't exactly clean.

I took a moment to remove and discard them.

Not one of my finest moments.

I also took off my jacket and threw it behind some rocks. No amount of dry cleaning would erase the memory of Harvey and Turbo hurling on it.

Another glance down that tunnel told me that it was time to go.

Whatever was down there, it wasn't bound to be a good thing, but it was the best chance I had of me making it back to my crew in one piece. If I ran back outside, I'd be flamed, and without Griff's shield to help protect me...well, I didn't want to think about it.

"Let's do this, Ian," I said after taking a calming breath. "What's the worst that can happen?"

In response, I heard a distant roar, followed by a scream, followed by a crunch.

"Huh," I said, thinking that maybe going outside might just be the better plan.

A few steps back toward the entrance changed my mind on that, though.

The three dragons were flying back toward the cave I was in and I had no means of causing an avalanche like the mages did. And if those silly birds were flying back after me, I could only assume that my mages did a bang-up job on blocking the cave they'd escaped to. A quick zoom verified that their cave was indeed crumbled.

It was time to make a run for it.

"If you make it out of here alive, you're going to take a refresher course on geography," I hissed an instant before I started down the hill that headed deeper into the darkness.

CHAPTER 15

J knew the dragons wouldn't be able to get down the tunnel in their bird form, but even in their human shape they were known to be deadly. They weren't considered the rulers of the Badlands for nothing.

But if memory served, demons ruled the deeper levels. Or was it that….

Nope. Try as I might, I just couldn't remember what the hell that third creature was called. Nothing came to mind in the form of an image either.

I continued making my way down the hill until a haze of light began radiating below.

The third creature I was trying to remember was some kind of lizard or snake. That *sounded* about right, anyway, but without a name or a face to go with it, I wasn't 100% certain. Chances were that my mind was just searching for anything at this point. Pretty soon it'd start suggesting that there was some Netherworld pixie that was more fierce than demons.

"Wait," I said, worried. "That's *not* it, right?"

I shook my head. No, it couldn't be. There was something else. It was deadly or clever or ruthless or…something.

That was dumb. Obviously it was deadly. If it weren't, how could it rule the deeper levels? Assuming it did. Something told me that demons were still the top of the chart down here. Maybe.

Gah!

"He's gone this way," I heard a voice say from behind me.

"No shit, asshole," another voice replied. "Where else could he have gone?"

"Shut up."

Great, so they were on my tail faster than I'd expected. I had to pick up my pace.

Dragons behind me and hell below.

Perfect.

"My point is that we were caught off his trail by the soiled underpants and suit jacket he'd put behind the rocks."

"Oh, right."

I frowned and continued moving forward. Obviously they could pick up my scent easily enough. Not that the scent I left behind was all that difficult to track. Regardless, trying to hide in a crevice as they walked on by was likely an exercise in futility.

Then again, I *could* just wait them out and unleash Boomy on them. That would be easy, actually.

"Make sure to keep your protective plating up," said one of them. "He has that infernal weapon with him."

So much for that.

The heat was increasing with each step down into the abyss. I guess this made sense considering I was effectively walking down to hell, in a non-metaphorical sense. I mean, it's not like the hell that people think they'll spend an eternity in or anything, but I wouldn't be surprised if *that* hell was based on this one. It smelled of sulfur, there were beasts and demons down here, and if you weren't careful, you'd end up in a pit of fire, get captured and tortured, and/or become the meal of some creature that would devour you slowly over many days.

Fun stuff.

"He's not too far ahead," one of the dragons said, signaling me to pick up my pace.

The light was brightening, so I was getting closer and closer to the first circle.

Ah hah! The basic geography of the nine levels came flooding back. So schooling wasn't wasted on me, after all.

The word "circle" had triggered the memory, and that led me to the name "Dante," the poet who wrote about the journey through hell.

He got one thing right: There were nine circles, assuming you went all the way through to the bottom of the place….Something I had no intention of doing.

That's about where his accuracy failed, though.

In Dante's rendition, each level represented a sin archetype: limbo, lust, gluttony, greed, wrath, heresy, violence, fraud, and treachery. These were drilled into our heads in class because they were essentially correct, just not in the way Dante thought. He pictured them as rings where those who served the various manifestations of the sins would spend their eternities, subjected to incessant torment. In reality, each level represented those things due to the beings who ruled said level, as they held those particular habits in high regard. There was no "sin" about it, just monsters doing what they did naturally.

This was perfect because I had no intention of going down through all of those levels. I just wanted to get to the tunnel that led to the cave my team was in. Once we were back together, we'd head to Charlotte's tower, get Warren back, and return to the Overworld.

Fortunately, I was on level one, which meant that

everything here was just hanging out. They were slow, complacent, and couldn't give two shits about anything.

Giant slugs.

Sure, they were goopy and grotesque. I mean, imagine your average slug, but ten feet tall. Think of the trail of slime that sucker would leave and you've got the general idea of what my first step onto level one felt like.

And that meant I was destroying yet another pair of dress shoes.

Why did I even bother to look nice?

"I heard a footstep press into the muck," said one of the dragons. "He's on the level. Let's go!"

No more time to plan.

I picked up my pace, though it felt like I was running on an icy surface. Using this to my advantage, I ran toward an angled area and began sliding down like I was on a skateboard.

Unfortunately, this didn't last too long because the slime started to build up until it covered my shoe. This slowed my pace considerably, but it didn't stop me.

What *did* stop me was a massive slug. The thing made a loud whining sound as I slammed into its side and bounced off.

I landed right in a massive pile of slug-gel.

It was all I could do not to lose my lunch as I spat out the bitter-tasting substance and wiped it from my eyes. Honestly, it was like I'd fallen into an enormous jar of petroleum jelly.

When I'd finally cleared my eyes of the gunk, I looked up to see the slug's eye-stalks looking straight down at me.

This just wasn't my day.

CHAPTER 16

I went for Boomy but it just slipped out of my hands like a wet bar of soap. Honestly, it was worse than zombie goop.

"Why did you strike me?" a voice said.

My eyes shot wide open.

"You can talk?"

"Not like you, no," the slug replied. "I am using telepathy. Were I to use regular speech, you would not understand me."

"But you can understand me?" I asked and then realized that I wasn't speaking aloud either. "Oh. Wicked."

"You have no idea," it said flatly. "Now, why did you strike me?"

"Oh, sorry about that. I'm being chased by dragons and—"

"We do not like dragons," the slug interrupted, moving one of its eye-stalks to look up in the direction from whence I came. "Can you breathe in the essence?"

"The what?"

"That which you are lying in."

Its left eye was focused on the hill I'd slid down, but the other one moved to point at the jelly I was in.

"Ah. No, not a chance."

"How long can you hold your breath?"

"A minute or two, I guess. Why?"

"That will have to do," the slug said and then began sliding toward me. "You may wish to begin now."

"Oh, shit," I said, gulping in a lungful of air before its massive body covered me.

It wasn't as heavy as I'd expected, but I certainly had no desire to meet my doom in this situation.

"What the hell are you doing?" I asked as I fought to slow my heart rate.

"Protecting you from the dragons. They are coming. Remain silent."

I didn't want to remain silent, but what was I going to do? If I kept pestering the thing, it'd either turn me over to the dragons and be done with me or it'd take too long to shoo my hunters away. In either case, I'd be a goner, so I kept my mouth—or brain—shut and focused on staying calm.

"You there!"

It was one of the dragons. I couldn't actually *hear* it speaking, but apparently the slug was channeling everything around it through to me. Maybe it was because we were connected physically? I had no way of knowing, but I listened.

"Yes," replied the slug.

"We're looking for a human that came through here," the dragon said. "It looks to have slid directly to this spot, in fact."

"Yes," the slug said.

I could feel the anger welling up in the dragon. "Where the hell did he go?"

"Speak or we will gut you where you stand," said another dragon.

The slug was not afraid, which was quite impressive.

Actually, this entire ordeal was pretty incredible. How was I able to hear this conversation and feel the emotions of those around the slug? One thing was for certain, I was never going to look at the little guys the same way again when I saw them in the rain.

All of the dragons pulled out swords.

How did I know this?

"Answer us now or we will slice you in two," the main dragon said in a voice laced with venom. "Where is the human?"

I had the distinct impression that the slug's eye-stalks had turned to point away from its current location.

"He went that-a-way."

"Good."

The blades all went back into their sheaths and the dragons ran away.

A few moments later, the slug moved off of me and I fought to pull in as much oxygen as possible. I didn't want to be too loud because it may have attracted the dragons back to our position, so every time I coughed I had to stick my head back in the goop.

Lovely.

"Where did you send them?" I asked after a few moments.

Its stalks moved to point in the direction that they'd gone.

"Where does that lead?"

"It circles around and returns about halfway up to the surface from the direction you came," he replied. "They will return in about ten minutes."

Damn. I was hoping I could run right back out to the surface and cross over to the cave where my team was. Chances were that I couldn't get in there anyway, but it would have put some distance between me and the dragons.

Then I realized that they weren't going to be all that pleased with the slug for leading them astray.

"They'll kill you," I said, feeling equally terrible and amazed how the thing risked its life for me like that. "You have to get out of here."

"I do not fear death," it said without inflection. "But I will be gone before they return. Unlike you, I can control my slide along the essence." It then turned one of its eyes toward me. "You, however, must leave before they return. I cannot protect you twice."

"Right. True," I said, getting up and wiping the goop from my head. "Any suggestions on where I should go?"

"Down."

I swallowed hard.

"Any other suggestions?"

"No." It clearly sensed my trepidation. "You are seeking a connection to the tunnel network, yes?"

"I... Yeah. How'd you know that?"

"Your mind is quite open," it replied. "The connection point is at the lowest point in the nine levels. You must traverse each level in order to reach your goal."

It spun around and began sliding away.

"Wait," I called out. "How do I get to the next level?"

The slug came to a stop and moved its eye-stalks to point toward a dark area off to its right.

"There," it said. "In the darkness resides a winding set of stairs. Each level has these. They are on opposite sides as you go down."

"So no elevator?"

Its stalks crossed. "Sorry?"

"Nothing. So I have to take the stairs to go down to the next level, then?"

I more stated this than asked it. Clearly the slug understood that the question was rhetorical, because it merely said, "Good luck."

"Thanks," I replied, "and thanks for helping me out. I really appreciate it."

"No need," said the slug as it spun and began sliding away. "I shall do anything to thwart the wretchedness of a dragon."

It disappeared and I saw the line of "essence" close over behind it, covering its escape. That was pretty cool.

Knowing that the dragons would return soon, I carefully picked up Boomy and set off toward the darkness.

The stairs were at the back of the wall. They were made of a concrete-like substance, and the entry was tight. I was slipping and sliding because of the damn goop. I fell on my ass more than once while trying to use my arms against the walls to hold me up. Finally, I reached what I could only imagine was the halfway point to the next level. This was apparent because the goop dried up. A couple steps more and I felt the sensation of the "essence" pulling away from my clothes, hair, and flesh. I stood there until it was all gone.

At least there was one benefit of going down a level.

I continued down and began walking toward the glow of reddish light in front of me.

This was the level of lust.

I grinned and boldly walked out like I owned the place.

CHAPTER 17

*N*ow, you may think that this level would be covered with succubi and incubi.

It was not.

Running around on this level were a bunch of satyr. Yep, I'm talking about the beasts with horse-like ears and tails, though some looked more like goats to me. They had erections that made one wonder if little blue pills were considered daily vitamins in these parts.

Fortunately, none of them had seen me yet. They were all too busy "enjoying" each other, and from the looks of it, they didn't seem to care if their partner was male or female.

I slunk back into the shadows just as a satyress walked in from one of the side tunnels.

She was exceptionally attractive and had a great rack that was unveiled for the world to see, but the fact that she also had the body of a goat from the waist down was rather a turn off.

No amount of blue pills would change my mind on that fact.

It was fine for the satyrs, obviously, because they were all of the same ilk. Plus, it was clear that they would put their oversized pokers in anything. As a case in point, one of them was busily screwing a hole in the wall.

My biggest worry was that they'd all kill to have something *different* to treat as a love-toy.

One thing was for sure, I was glad all that petroleum jelly stuff had disappeared.

Then again, if they caught me, maybe not.

I seriously had to be careful.

The walls were smooth on this side of the level and it hung mostly in the shadows. But I didn't know how good their sense of smell was, or if their eyes were as adept as mine. The only thing I could do was keep moving as swiftly and quietly as possible.

My slug pal from level one said that the tunnels that connected to each level were on opposite sides, so I had to get across without being busted…literally.

I zoomed my vision and saw that the tunnel on the opposite side was a pretty good trek from my current position. The one on the first level wasn't so bad because of the connection point from the surface, and because I had been able to slide across using slug essence. This level didn't have such a thing.

I would have expected to see just as much essence here, though of a different kind.

There wasn't any.

Frankly, that was a relief. My shoes had already been through enough. Besides…ew.

Everything was going smoothly until a waft of air blew in from all of the tunnels. Why this happened, I don't know, but it stirred up animal dander and threw it right in my face.

Now, I wasn't one who generally had to deal with allergies, but apparently horse or goat hair didn't sit well with my nasal passages.

I squeezed my nose with everything I had as I tried to fight back the urge.

You see, I'm not one of those people who can sneeze quietly. I'm the type who can wake the dead. And to make matters even more fun, my sneezes always come in packages of three. That's three big-ass sneezes that would most definitely attract the attention of boner-wielding goat-people.

It was no use, my sinuses and lungs were in revolt and there wasn't a damn thing I could do about it.

I sneezed.

The sound of satyr playtime stopped.

I sneezed again.

Heads turned my way.

I sneezed again.

"What is that?" said one of the males, using his pork-sword to point in my direction.

"I don't know," said a female, "but surely it is new to the area?"

The male nodded. "I agree, and I like it when you call me Shirley."

That was a different take on an old joke, though I don't think it was intended as humor.

With a bunch of satyrs and satyresses looking my way, I had a choice to make. I could either make a run for it, which would probably just entice them more, or I could step out and try to communicate, hoping they would assist me.

I stepped out.

"Oh," said the female, "he is rather gorgeous. I call dibs."

"And I have seconds," hollered the male.

Within moments, a line had formed. I wanted to swallow hard, but the connotation of the act, and potential miscommunication that went along with it, kept me from doing so.

The female clomped up to me and traced my face with her finger.

"You may have me now," she said with sparkling eyes.

"Uh," I choked, feeling exceedingly uncomfortable. "Listen, babe…you're, like, really pretty and all that, but I'm a vegetarian."

"So am I," she replied with a tilt of her head. "We all are."

Damn. That didn't work.

"Right…uh…" A flash of brilliance struck. "I'm also impotent."

She frowned. "Oh. Well then, I guess only the males get to have fun with you."

"Fuck," I hissed.

"That's the idea," said the male who had walked up at my admission of being incapable of using my naughty bits.

He was smiling like a guy who'd seen his first nudie magazine and his hoozitwhatsit poked my arm.

"Nasty," I said, yanking my arm away. "I'm not into dudes, dude."

He laughed. "That doesn't matter."

"It doesn't?"

"Not to me."

"Oh…Oh!" I pressed my back against the wall. "Not cool, man."

My mind was racing as I grabbed hold of Boomy, making sure not to touch the satyr's junk in the process.

I didn't have enough breaker bullets for them all, but maybe I could keep them at bay if they saw what Boomy was capable of. Besides, assuming I got through this level, I still had seven more to go and I was sure I'd need plenty of bullets to make it all the way out.

What I needed was a diversion. Something that…

The dragons.

"Hey," I said, releasing Boomy and holding up my hands, "how do you guys feel about dragons?"

Their faces grew dark.

Good.

"Their kind are an abomination," said the male who was standing in front of me.

"I couldn't agree more," I replied with much enthusiasm. "Ever boned one?"

"What?"

"A dragon. Have you ever boned one?"

They were all looking around at each other. My question had clearly confused them.

The lead male furrowed his brow. "We have not."

"Want to?"

More glances were exchanged. Their dark looks were slowly morphing into faces of sinister interest.

"I can see the prospect excites you," I said quickly, "and I happen to have some insider information regarding dragons that you probably don't know about."

"What is it?" said the satyress I had disappointed earlier.

"All dragons have a secret fantasy to be in an orgy with satyrs and satyresses."

"They do?" came the communal response.

"Who wouldn't?" I asked, and then quickly added, "except for me, of course. I'm...uh...asexual."

All their heads tilted at the word.

"That means that I don't have sex like you guys do." An idea hit. "In fact, if you were to attempt relations with me, all of your danglies would fall off."

They all took a step back as a sound of "whoa" filled the room.

"That's right. It'd be a shame, too, since you guys seriously like using those things."

As a test, I stepped toward them and they backed farther

away. That would probably suffice in giving me safe passage to the next level, but I still needed to keep the dragons busy for a while.

"Anyhoo, there are three dragons following me," I explained. "They'll be coming down those steps any moment now."

"Why are they following you?"

"Because they'd asked if I knew how to get to the level where the satyrs and satyresses live."

This seemed to confuse them even more. That was likely due to the fact that dragons ruled the Badlands, which meant that they knew exactly which creature lived on each level that sat in their lands.

I had to recover from that.

"They're new to the area," I said. "All of them were born in the Overworld. This is their first trip here. They'd heard all about you guys from the, uh, tourist pamphlets."

"Tourist pamphlets?" the male replied as his engorged member bounced around as if seeking something to keep it occupied.

"Exactly." I glanced into the darkness where the stairs were that led back to level one and saw three bodies walking out. "Anyway, they're on their way in now and I'm sure they'd love to meet you all."

As one, the creatures spun and cast their lusting eyes on the three dragons who had just walked into their midst.

"What's going on here?" said the main dragon, glaring at me.

"These are the satyrs you asked about," I called back. "The ones in the pamphlet. They'd be happy to include you in their orgy—right, gang?"

"Delighted," said the lead satyr.

"With pleasure," agreed that satyress.

The dragons laughed in a not-so-funny way. It was

obvious they were on to my ruse, but they also seemed to be somewhat apprehensive.

"Very clever, human," said the main dragon. "Unfortunately, your plan won't work. We are the rulers of this land." She turned her gaze back toward the half-animals. "You will not be having sex with us."

The goat-people looked instantly bummed out.

The dragon then pointed in my direction. "I demand that you bring this man to me."

The lead goat-dude's eyes went wide. "But he can make our dicks fall off."

"He can what?"

"It's true," I called out. "I can."

"How?" asked the dragon.

I stuck my tongue out at her. "That's for me to know and for you to find out."

"What are you, five years old?" She didn't wait for an answer. Instead, she stepped forward. "If you do not bring that man to me right now, I shall send a scourge upon your people that will do far worse than remove your genitalia." Then she grinned evilly. "If you *do* retrieve him and your penises fall off, I shall send healing that will not only replace your fallen appendages, but they will be even larger than they are now."

Shit.

Dragons were clearly better at deception than me.

I turned and ran.

CHAPTER 18

There was no way I could outrun even one of these damn things, and I was pretty fast.

I would have loved to employ *Haste* right about now, but that would mean I'd have to stop, take a deep breath, get into a semi-meditative state, and trigger the skill. There was no time for that. If I shut my eyes at this point, I'd either be captured by the satyrs behind me or boned by the ones I was heading toward.

To make matters worse, the satyrs behind me yelled out to the ones ahead that I was to be captured.

Now, if you can imagine a bunch of goat-dudes bolting at you with raging tallywackers bouncing around like pogo sticks, you'll get the general idea of the trepidation I was feeling.

There was no way I could let these horny bastards catch me, so I did the only thing that made any sense.

I whipped out Boomy and shot off one of their dicks.

The poor beast unleashed the most horrific scream I'd ever heard. Then it keeled over and died.

That was something to put in the "how to kill a satyr" filing cabinet.

To end a vampire, you shoot it in the heart or head with a wood-infused bullet, or you can drive a wooden stake into its heart. Same gig with a werewolf, but you used silver instead of wood.

Satyrs? Blow their cocks off.

Sounded wrong, but taken in context it was the correct way to destroy one of the horny creatures.

And it worked, but I didn't have enough bullets to match the number of throbbing pipes in the room.

Fortunately, they'd all stopped at seeing their comrade lying lifeless in their shared essence. Their faces were a mix between shock and terror. This worked in my favor, seeing that I still had Boomy drawn and was waving it toward all of their mid-sections as I briskly walked toward the dark tunnel that housed the stairs leading down to level three.

"Stop him," yelled the dragon.

The satyrs shook their heads in unison.

"I'll kill you all," the dragon warned in a voice that was laced with dread. "Imagine all of your appendages falling off at the snap of my fingers."

I stopped. It was one thing to be deceptive, but it was quite another to strike terror into the hearts of people—or goat-people, as the case may be—just because you could. Dragons could do minor magic. I knew this. Everyone knew this. But to state that they could snap their fingers and have everyone's personal eggplant disappear was just ludicrous. Not even my mages could manage that on such a scale, and they were some of the most advanced mages around.

"Wait a second," I called out to the dragon, who was sufficiently far away. "First off, what's your name?"

She looked at me apprehensively. "Claire. Why?"

"Because I don't want to keep thinking of you as 'lead

dragon,'" I answered. "I'm assuming you *are* the leader of these other two idiots."

The other dragons frowned, but Claire grinned.

"Yes," she answered. "This is Wilbur and this is Stan."

"Great names for dragons," I said with a chuckle. "Obviously your mother has quite the creative mind."

"Thank you," said Claire with a nod. "I'll be sure to let her know that those were your final words."

I raised an eyebrow. "Except that they won't be my final words."

"She won't know that. Now, what is it you want?"

"Right." I held up Boomy and looked at it. "Everyone here has just seen that I can blow off any cock in here quite easily."

There were a bunch of interested looks at my comment. See? That wording just wasn't going to work.

I groaned. "I'm talking about the removal of your peckers by firing my gun at them."

Their interested looks fell away.

"Exactly." Honestly, I felt almost like a saint compared to these horny fuckers. "Anyway, the point is that while I've demonstrated my capability, I think you're bluffing."

Claire tilted her head at me and I saw a moment of hesitation in her eyes. I'd just put her into the awkward position of having to prove herself, and I knew damn well she couldn't.

Dragons were nothing but bullies. As long as people believed their hype, the fear would keep everyone in line, doing their bidding. But when someone stood up to them and knocked them on their asses, that hype turned to reality and people got pissed.

"What are you saying?" Claire asked in a cold voice.

"I'm saying that you're full of shit," I replied, which elicited a gasp from the satyrs. "If your magic is so great, why are you having to chase me? Why can't you just cast a spell and lock me in place?"

All satyr heads turned toward Claire.

"It's not how we do things," she replied smoothly. "To do so would go against the balance of what we have promised our servants."

I cackled at that as the satyrs turned back to me.

"You guys really *are* a piece of work," I stated. "You've hooked these poor creatures so deeply into your lies that they react purely out of fear. You have no more ability to do magic than I do."

"We most certainly can do magic," argued Wilbur.

"So can I, but neither of us can cast spells to the degree you three are claiming."

Stan pushed out his chest. "Can too."

I looked around and saw a line of goat-dudes blocking the exit, which was only about one hundred feet away at this point. At my standard speed of running, I could hit that in seconds, but only if those satyrs were out of my way.

Time for Claire to put her money where her mouth was. If she could really do what she said, then those satyrs would be gone; if she couldn't, the dragons were about to find out what being the focus of an orgy felt like.

"Okay, then," I said, crossing my arms. "Prove it."

The dragons glanced at each other.

"How?"

"Oh, I don't know," I replied, chewing my lip as if in thought. I then casually spun around and pointed at the only satyrs blocking my path. "Snap your fingers and make their dicks fall off."

The satyrs didn't like this idea. In fact, one of them slowly stepped away from the others, melding itself into the shadow that hung over the opposite wall.

"I don't need to prove anything to you, human."

"That's what I thought," I teased. "You can't do it." I then spun and threw my hands up in the air. "See, my newfound satyr friends? The dragons have nothing but bravado! They've been tricking you all of these years and you've fallen for it because they're *very* good at bullying others. But it's all…hot air."

At that proclamation, Claire snapped her fingers.

I spun and saw the satyrs' dongs drop off.

I wasn't expecting that, but it *did* clear the way to the stairwell since those poor bastards all hit the ground, dead, an instant later.

"Now," commanded Claire, "get him before I do that to the rest of you!"

They didn't need to be told again.

I took off for the stairs while still wondering why the dragons didn't just fire off some crazy spell at me. There had to be a reason for it, but I didn't have a clue what it could be.

One thing was for sure, though, they weren't going to fall for my bullshit on level three. That meant I had to make it through that one well ahead of them.

I nearly fell down the stairs as the sounds of panting satyrs filled the upper steps, stopping at the mid-point, disallowed to go any farther.

There was no time to rest, though. The dragons would be right behind me, once the boner-wielding goat-people cleared a path. Right now they were all smashed together and there was plenty of grunting going on. Seriously, I was feeling downright pious in comparison to those creatures.

I sighed.

Level three was dead ahead and it was the circle of gluttony.

That meant manticores.

CHAPTER 19

*A*h, manticores. Don't ya just love 'em? The head of a human, the body of a lion, and a tail full of poisonous spines. They also had three rows of razor-sharp teeth that made sure no bones got left behind when they dined.

Favorite meal? Humanoids.

So while everyone on level two wanted to make me their personal blow-up doll, the beasties on this level would be more interested in having me for lunch.

Rather fitting for this level, I suppose.

I had no idea what filled them up down here, since it wasn't like the place was teeming with humans. There had to be something else they were eating because I heard a growl, a cry, and a chomp. It was the same type of cry I'd heard when coming in from the outside, but far louder this close. How it resonated all the way up the levels was beyond me. I assumed there were some type of holes or a vent or something that managed to carry sound waves.

Seeing that these were creatures who hunted, I assumed that my scent was going to be picked up soon enough.

I glanced up and saw a winged version of the manticores. It was far larger than the rest, having a golden mane, rippling muscles, and deep red eyes.

It was flying directly at me.

Either it was just doing its rounds or it knew I was standing there.

There was nowhere to run, either. If I went back up the steps, the dragons would snag me, or the satyrs would use me like a pincushion. If I ran out into level three, I'd end up on a silver serving dish with an apple in my mouth. And if I just stood here, it'd be a dice roll to see which fate I faced first.

Now seemed like a good time to employ one of my special abilities. And I would have done just that, had the damn winged manticore not landed directly in front of me and started padding forward.

"Hi there," I said with a petrified smile. "Nice weather we're having, eh?"

"You're a human."

"Got it in one," I replied, pointing at him and winking at the same time. "And you're a manticore. Quite a specimen, too, if I may say so."

Drool poured from his mouth as he ran a long tongue over his pointed teeth. "I haven't tasted human bones in a very long time."

"I'm sure the flavor hasn't changed." I gulped. "Tastes like chicken, right?"

"Never had chicken," he said as his eyes gazed at me as if I were the last remaining turkey leg at a holiday feast. "We only get rodents, changed manticores, and tofu down here."

That made me jolt.

"Tofu?"

"It's awful," he said. "Flavorless. Almost as bad as the rice cakes they used to give us."

"That sounds dreadful."

"Dragons," the manticore said with a sneer. "They suck."

"Couldn't agree more, my friend."

It took a step forward and sniffed me. Water filled the beast's eyes like it'd just taken a hit of heroin.

"I want this to last," it said as it showed all three rows of teeth to me.

Just as he lunged forward, I sidestepped him and stuck Boomy against his temple.

"All right, lion-boy," I said in a menacing voice, "I don't want to have to blow your brains out, but I will."

"What is that you have on my head?"

"A gun."

"A what?"

"A gun," I said again. "It's a weapon that contains projectiles. If I pull the trigger, the contents of your head will decorate the entire area here."

Its eyes creased, but it stayed looking forward.

"What do you want?"

"To get to the other side of this level without being eaten."

"Not possible."

"Then I guess I'll just have to shoot you," I stated without inflection.

"The others will still eat you."

"Yeah, but *you* won't," I pointed out, "and you'll be dead, too." He didn't respond, which let me know that he was weighing things. "I'll let you in on a little secret. There are three more humanoids chasing me."

"Three?"

"Three. If you fly me to the other side quickly, you can be back in time to pounce on them before anyone else has a chance."

"Hmmm." His eyes glanced in my direction, but his head didn't move. "How do I know you're speaking the truth?"

"You don't, but ask yourself why a human would risk running through the nine levels unless there was something chasing him?"

He nodded. "Valid point."

"Now, I'm going to climb onto your back and you're going to fly me over, okay?"

"I will do as you say."

As I was about to hop on, I looked back and saw that his tail was flaring. He was obviously planning on stabbing me in the back with his vicious spines once I was in place. I couldn't blame him. Four meals was better than three, after all.

"Now, now," I said, tapping the gun against his head. "I see your tail and I know your thoughts. If you so much as move those spines in my direction, your life will be forfeit." As a gesture of proof, I tapped Boomy's nozzle against his head again. "Are we clear?"

He grunted. "We are."

"Move out of the way, you idiots," I heard the voice of Claire calling out. "And keep your damn dicks off of me."

I fired Boomy up the stairs, allowing the ricochet to hopefully strike something.

This accomplished two things. First was a yelp and some bustling from above. Second was that the manticore's eyes grew very wide, clearly learning that I was not messing around regarding the power of the weapon I was wielding.

"You heard the humanoids," I whispered, "and you know what kind of power I have in my hand. So what's it going to be? Are you flying me over there or am I blowing your head off?"

It sniffed the air in the direction of the stairs. "Smells like balls up there."

"Not surprising."

The manticore glanced sideways at Boomy and sighed.
"Climb on."

CHAPTER 20

Of all the things that had happened today, this was the best, and that wasn't saying much.

Yes, I had to be careful that the damn thing wasn't going to try and stab me with its tail, but soaring over the rest of the beasties in the feeding frenzy below was far nicer than trying to traverse it on foot. I wouldn't have made it ten steps, Boomy or not.

Up here, though, I felt like nothing could touch me.

"I have to say that you've got it better than all those below you…" I paused. "What's your name, anyway?"

"Jim."

I was expecting "Gravelor" or "Croseidon" or something like that. Not "Jim."

"I'm Ian, Jim."

"Don't care."

"Right. Well, anyway, I was saying that you've got a pretty decent gig up here, Jim."

"Glad you think so," he replied as we turned a sharp corner that revealed another two manticores flying toward us.

"Uh...Jim...who are they?" I asked in an almost casual tone.

"My fellow rulers."

"That's not good for you, Jim," I said.

"For me?"

"Well, you *do* want to get back to those three humanoids, right? These guys are your competition, no?"

"Shit," Jim said with a growl. "You're right. Use your projectile launcher on them."

"It's called a gun, Jim."

"Don't care. Kill them."

I had to think about this for a second. If I pulled Boomy away from Jim's head, he could easily stab me with his tail before I had time to reengage. On the other hand, if the other flying manticores got much closer, they'd rake me off Jim anyway, and probably kill him in the process.

Fortunately, I always carried a spare gun, just in case.

I took it out with my left hand and stuck it on Jim's opposite temple.

"I have two of these, Jim, so don't get any ideas."

"You'd better kill them fast," Jim said almost desperately.

I fired Boomy and struck the first incoming lion-beast right between the eyes. It dropped like a lead balloon, falling with a splat on the ground below. The feeding frenzy that ensued was horrific.

The second flier hesitated at seeing this, keeping its distance.

"What is this devilry, Jim?" it said while casually flapping its wings.

"He's my new...friend," Jim replied.

"We're friends now?" I whispered with a laugh, thinking it unlikely that Jim and I would ever end up out at a pub throwing back a few beers.

"You know the rules," the other manticore said. "All food is communal, friends or not."

"Of course I know, Cleo," Jim replied with a venomous voice. "With Chelsie out of the way, though, you and I can set new rules. Ones that are befitting of the winged manticores, not the lowly walkers."

The names that these things had were simply *too* human. It kind of weirded me out. I'd met a few people over the years who didn't fit their names, but this was insanity.

"What do you have in mind, Jim?" Cleo asked.

"We shall become one," Jim replied, maintaining his position. "Our rule will be done with the power of six rows."

I assumed he meant rows of teeth, seeing as there weren't any rowboats around.

"You are proposing marriage?"

"Out of convenience only."

"Yet it still requires copulation," countered Cleo.

"I am aware," Jim said back.

Cleo frowned while studying him. She appeared completely baffled by Jim's suggestion. It was clear there was no love between them.

"But I thought you were only interested in male manticores, Jim?"

Jim's altitude dropped enough to cause me to constrict my legs around his waist.

"Why does everyone think that?" he asked. "I'm *not* gay. I just haven't found the right mate."

"Until now?" Cleo said, looking dubious.

"I marry for purpose, not love."

The two continued flapping their wings for a few quiet moments.

I honestly couldn't care less what ended up happening between the two of them. My bigger worry was that the dragons were bound to be coming through any second and then the shit was going to hit the fan. Once they spread the word as to who they truly were, Jim would recognize my ruse and do his damndest to end me, even at the expense of his own life.

"Fine," Cleo said finally. "We have an arrangement. Now, let us dine on this human together."

"I think not," I said, raising Boomy and pointing it at her. "You already saw what I did to your third-wheel manticore. I have no problem making my wedding gift to you be a similar fate."

"Do not fire at her," Jim said over his shoulder quietly. "It will only cause two of those below to morph into fliers."

I glanced down at all the hungry faces.

"What?"

"There must be no fewer than two rulers, though three is preferred," Jim explained. "If you kill Cleo, two more will rise in her place and we will have another battle to contend with. If Cleo and I marry, then we will supersede the law of three and may rule together without the third manticore."

"Only if we copulate," Cleo reminded him.

I felt Jim bristle at the thought. Maybe he *was* only into dude manticores? Not that I gave a shit one way or the other, but it just went to show that power was more important to him than his personal preferences.

"Let's go, Jim," I said, tapping him on the temple with the smaller gun as I kept Boomy trained on his new fiancée. "I need to get to the next level fast."

He swerved and headed toward the exit, covering the distance quickly as Cleo flew alongside us.

There were only a couple hundred feet left to go when a rumbling sound rippled through the manticores below.

Another ten seconds and I'd be home free.

"What is the bustle of noise?" said Jim as he continued his descent. "Something has the flock worried."

Five seconds.

"Dragons," said Cleo.

Three seconds.

"What?"

One second.

"Dragons have entered the area."

Jim stopped about ten feet above the ground.

"Dragons?" he yelled and then spun his head back at me. "You said they were humans!"

I licked my lips.

"Technically, Jim, I said they were humanoids."

Jim roared so loud that I nearly dropped Boomy.

"Kill him," he commanded as I dived off his back an instant before his tail would have struck me.

I hit the ground with a roll and dived into the darkness that led to the stairwell and scrambled down until I passed the halfway point.

"Son of a bitch," Jim was yelling from the top of the stairs. "I cannot believe I was fooled by that stupid human!"

"Great," said Cleo. "I'm marrying a moron."

CHAPTER 21

I'd made it to the level of greed. This could be a good thing or a bad thing.

I had money on my person, but it was Overworld money. Still, if I could somehow position it as being precious *because* it wasn't available for use on this plane, maybe the goblins who ruled this level would let me through without a fuss.

That was the good thing.

The bad thing was that dragons were known for having jewels that goblins drooled over.

I had to get there first.

Fortunately, the flying manticores known as Jim and Cleo were on *this* side of level three. Now, I knew that dragons can fly too, but there wasn't enough overhead in any of these circles to allow for creatures that big.

In other words, I had an edge.

Two, actually.

You see, I knew how to deal with goblins. They were greedy, sure, but they also were easily convinced if you showed strong bravado and adopted a New York accent. I'd learned this when Chief Michaels—the guy who ran the Las

113

Vegas PPD when I started there—had me ride with him to take down a small batch of goblins who had somehow escaped the Netherworld a number of years back. I was ready to go in with guns blazing, but Chief Michaels had me put the gun away and showed me how to handle goblins properly.

It was time for that lesson to pay out.

I stepped out into the light and found a bustling group of goblins all working tables, selling stuff to each other, and doing what they do best: haggling.

"Hey, buddy," I said in my best New Yorker accent to a goblin who was walking by, "come over here."

He stepped over and scanned me from head to toe.

I scanned him right back.

His face was pointed and wrinkled, laced with creases that surrounded a set of dull, angst-ridden eyes. His ears were pointy and long. All in all, he was what you'd expect a goblin to look like. Except for one thing. He was wearing a suit. A nice one, too. In fact, it was so nice that I nearly asked him who his tailor was, but I caught myself while remembering the situation I was in.

"Nice shoes, pal," the little guy said, "but you ain't got on no jacket. You're unfinished, yeah? Can't walk around like that in this world or you'll be eaten alive." He *tsk-tsk*'d. "They'll see you comin' a mile away, Jack."

"It's Ian, not Jack," I countered, "and I'd argue that it's the man who makes the suit, not the suit that makes the man."

"Good argument," he replied with a satisfied nod. Then he wiped his nose and said, "Whaddya want?"

Here's where I had to be careful.

He couldn't know that I had a couple of dragons after me or he'd definitely hold me up and collect a reward. Dragons may be ruthless but, as Claire had pointed out, they would follow the agreed upon rules and precepts they'd set up for their subjects. That meant Claire would be willing to pay for my capture.

"Heading down to level five," I said, whipping out a twenty. "You'll get one of these now and three more when we get to the other side, if you lead me there."

"Human money ain't worth nothin' here."

I stretched the bill between my hands and held it at eye level to him. "It ain't?"

He swallowed.

"Get me to the other side double-time and I'll even give ya one of these babies." I pulled out a fiver and showed it to him. "Can't find these easy in the Overworld. They're rare, I tell ya."

It wasn't true, of course, but he didn't know that.

"How rare?" he asked, studying the bill carefully.

"Only a hundred of 'em in existence."

His eye twitched.

"I've also got a one here," I said, showing him a green bill with George Washington's face on it. "It's the *only* one you'll ever find."

He licked his lips. "Is that why it has the number one on it?"

"You got it, pal," I replied before tucking all the money back in my wallet. "Obviously you're no dummy."

"That's true."

"So, whaddya say? We got a deal or what?"

He squinted and rubbed his chin as if he was thoroughly considering things, and this is when I channeled Chief Michaels.

"You know it makes sense, pal. Every second that swings past is a second wasted." I then stood tall and leaned away from him. "Of course, I could just snag one of these other enterprising—"

"All right, all right," he said, looking perturbed. "Let's go.

But keep up with me, I don't want to have to drag you along." He stopped and spun on me. "And no wise guy moves or I'll gut ya, see?"

For a guy who only came up to my waist, he was somewhat intimidating. But I met his glare with one of my own.

"A deal's a deal, pal," I stated as if it were written in stone. It wasn't. I was more than happy to kick him in the nards and run like hell, should it come to that. But he didn't know it. "When a Dex shakes hands on something, it means somethin'."

With that, the goblin blew his nose into his hand and held it out for a shake.

This was the equivalent of little kids spit-swearing. Ah, yes, that age-honored ritual of spitting in your hand, waiting for the other kid to do the same, and then shaking on an agreement. Honestly, it made me wonder how far we'd truly evolved from monkeys. I suppose we didn't throw shit at each other when irritated. We did worse, but at least there wasn't shit involved...usually.

I feigned snorting into my own hand and then, with bile building in my throat, shook his.

"What's your name?" I asked as I proceeded to wipe his snot off on the shoulder of his suit. "Not a fan of doing business with people I don't know."

"Renny," he said. "Renny Pache."

That was better than the manticores, anyway.

"Good to meet ya, Renny," I said and then motioned ahead. "Lead on."

CHAPTER 22

*O*f all the levels I'd been to thus far, this one I could get behind. Everybody wanted something out of everybody, sure, but there was an air of complexity to it that was different from the levels above.

These people had a moral code. Not a great one, mind you, but one nonetheless.

They sought the deal, and that meant something.

I doubt they had any compass regarding the classic example of it's-a-good-deal-if-everyone-comes-out-happy, of course. Hell, I'd bet Renny would sell me out in two-shakes for a better gift, regardless if the purchaser was a dragon or a werewolf. Goblins only cared about the better deal. They'd probably take living over gold, but that's because it was the best of two choices. If I remembered correctly, they even had a saying that talked about the logic of it. Something about how ten gold and dead means you only get ten gold, but no gold and alive means you could bust your hump and make way more than ten gold. It was basic math. But if death wasn't on the table, my dollar bills would pale in comparison to what Claire had up her sleeve, and you know damn well she'd have something to trade.

Renny was a fast little dude. I didn't have any trouble keeping up with him, but since every goblin within sight was wearing a suit that was similar to his, I could see the potential of looking away for a second and then accidentally following the wrong one.

That's when I saw the smear of snot on his shoulder.

The bile came back and I wished for a squirt of hand sanitizer.

Anyway, fact was that he'd been tagged because of my hand-wiping move and that made him easier to spot.

"Hey, big boy," said a particularly grotesque goblin who was wearing a pink nightie. "Want to come to my room for a…sample?"

"I…uh…"

Renny grabbed my wrist and dragged me away.

Okay, so "dragged" is a strong word. I would have leapfrogged ten or twenty of these little creatures had Renny not come to my aid.

"Keep your eyes on the prize," he said. "I got a meeting in twenty and I don't want to be held up on account of you trying to score some love-time, got it?"

"Got it," I replied, wondering if he actually thought I would have been interested anyway.

"Hey, pal," said another goblin who stepped in front of me, effectively blocking my path, "you need something? How about a nice radio?"

"Radio?"

"Back off, dicknose," Renny said, giving a shove to the other goblin. "This one's already got a deal going with me."

"Okay, okay," said Dicknose, which I hoped wasn't really his name. Although, to be fair, that was probably a fine name down here. "Just trying to make a living."

Renny guided me to a spot on the side where there weren't any tables.

"Look," he said, pointing at me, "quit staring at all the tables and wares, yeah? I told ya before that I got a meeting to get to." He pulled out a watch that was affixed to a gold chain. "We'll be there in two minutes if you can keep your head in the game."

I held my hands out in apology.

"You're right, pal," I said as a bell rang. "Let's go."

He grabbed my wrist and held me in place. I was actually surprised by his strength.

"What's going on?"

"Raid."

"You have roaches down here?"

Renny's brow furrowed. "What?"

"Never mind," I said, realizing it was a lame joke. "You guys get raided?"

"Only when something is out of place," he answered while looking around. Then he slowly turned and looked up at me. "Or someone," he added.

Shit.

"Okay, Renny," I said, dropping to his height, "I'm going to level with you. There are three dragons chasing me." I cracked open my billfold. "I've got a whole bunch of bills in this wallet if you're still willing to get me to those stairs."

His eyes glittered.

In a dull voice, he said, "I could probably get jewels for turning you in."

I then pulled out Boomy and stuck it in his side.

He nodded slowly.

"Better to live and get more gold, than to die with only a little bit," he said as a goblin who knew the motto well. "All right, I'll do it. Put the damn gun away, though. I don't like working like that."

The problem, as I saw it, was getting through the mass of goblins who were trying to spot what the hell was going on.

I stuck out like a sore thumb, too, being that I was much larger than even their staunchest specimen.

But that's when Renny did something I couldn't have expected.

He pulled out a large red card and held it high.

"VIP coming through," he shouted. "The alarms you're hearing are for this VIP. Clear the way, ya mongrels!"

The goblin crowd parted faster than a satyress's legs at an orgy.

We got to the stairs without a fuss, but now I was concerned that Renny was going to get screwed over even worse by the dragons. I probably shouldn't have cared, but that's just the kind of guy I was.

"Aren't you going to get in a lot of trouble for helping me?"

"Nope," he said, holding out his hand for payment.

I handed over the bills, as promised.

"Why not?"

"Because this is how we roll on level four, pal," he said while rubbing the currency between his fingers. "Deals are what we do. You made a deal with me, it's my responsibility to see it through."

"Yeah, but the dragons—"

"Won't do shit," he interrupted. "They're the ones who set up the rules. If they hurt me for upholding a contract, there'll be a revolt."

"Oh, well, thanks then."

"Don't mention it, pal." Renny turned to go and then stopped again. "Hey, listen, I probably shouldn't say anything, but level five has the faceless ones. If you want to get through there alive, you're going to need to know one simple trick."

I opened my wallet to show him it was empty. I had nothing left to bargain with.

"I'll take the gun," he said.

"Boomy?"

"Sure."

"Not a chance," I said, holding the Desert Eagle like it was my only child. Then I grabbed my back up. "How about this one?"

"Good enough," he said, snatching it out of my hand. He eyed it while grinning. "All right, so I can't tell you outright, but I will say this: What you don't see, can't hurt you."

I cocked my head to the side. "I don't get it."

"Best I can do, pal," he said before merging back into the flow of goblins.

Out in the distance I saw Claire and her two brothers making their way through the crowd. Why they didn't have a red card, I couldn't say, but I was glad they didn't.

It was time for me to visit the faceless ones.

CHAPTER 23

*R*enny's little tidbit of advice seemed to be worth a lot less than what I paid for it.

And it was bullshit anyway.

"What you don't see can't hurt you," he'd said.

Tell that to a sniper, the bogey man, a land mine, heart disease, radiation, Rachel when she was really pissed off at you but didn't say a fucking word about it until you'd turned your back and then she just lets loose and…

I coughed lightly, realizing that I was kind of letting myself get into a frenzy for no reason.

Or was there a reason?

I *was* in the realm of the faceless ones down here, and that meant level five. This was the level of wrath. I'd have to keep myself in check.

Anyway, the point was that there were plenty of things out there that you can't see but can sure as hell hurt you.

Every fiber of my being told me that it'd be better if I didn't walk out into the circle of "hell" I was standing in. Standing back here in the shadows would be super fine. Honestly, the thought of walking out into the open made me consider just surrendering to the dragons, and I probably would have if it weren't for the fact that my crew was out there and I needed to get to them.

They'd survive without me. I knew that. I wasn't *that* egotistical, after all. That wasn't the point, though. They were my responsibility, and that meant I had to do whatever I could to get to them...get to Rachel.

"Honor slays deceit," hissed a dark voice that was just outside of the entrance. "Love is for fools."

I felt a wave of cold running over my body. It made me shiver uncontrollably, as if I'd just fallen through a sheet of ice into the water below.

And what was that "Love is for fools" bit all about?

"Hate cures the disease of love," came another hiss, but this one sounded slightly different.

"Tried that once," I whispered to myself. "Didn't work."

Fortunately, there was no response to that.

"What you don't see, can't hurt you," played in my head again.

Dumb.

How could anyone actually believe that?

I was stalling.

"Well, Ian," I said to myself in a quiet voice, "you've gotten past goopy slugs, fucking (pun intended) satyrs, toothy manticores, and greedy goblins." I breathed out nervously. "If you get through this one unscathed, you'll only have to deal with demons, valkyries, fae, and that other thing that I was hoping you would have said as I rattled off the rest."

Damn it. Whatever that final thing was, it just wouldn't get to the surface of my brain. I wasn't even getting one of those "it's on the tip of my tongue" situations.

"Time to step out and face the faceless."

That felt like the wrong thing to say.

On instinct, I reached for Boomy but then remembered

that bullets would do nothing against these things. They were wisps, blank, void, wraith-like creatures that couldn't be killed with projectiles or standard battle tactics. Fact was that I couldn't say exactly *how* they could be destroyed. What I *did* know was that they could end me. Seemed a bit unfair, truth be told, but that's life in "hell."

I gathered my courage and took a step out beyond the mist.

There weren't many of them, but even one was more than enough.

My angst increased every time I looked at one of them, but I couldn't help myself. They floated like ghosts, wearing gray cloaks that hung on their frail-looking frames. I couldn't see their faces under the hoods, but seeing that they were known as the faceless ones, I doubted I'd spot anything discernible anyway.

One of them jolted and then spun toward me.

Sure enough, nothing was hidden in the opening of that cloak besides a somewhat oval shape that was only a shade or two lighter in gray than the cloak.

My blood began to boil for some reason.

Hate welled up in me.

"You're worthless, Ian," I yelled at myself as other voids joined and stared at me. "How could you leave your crew like that? What the hell were you thinking? Have you no honor?"

An instant later the barrel of my beloved Boomy was pressed against my own temple.

"Yes," came the hisses from all around me, sweeping my body to the core with freezing pain.

My finger ached to the pull the trigger as the self-loathing increased to the point of unbearableness.

Then I closed my eyes.

CHAPTER 24

The emotion fled and I lowered Boomy in a controlled fashion.

"See us," demanded the whispering voices, but I kept my eyes closed.

Apparently, Renny's advice was right. It wasn't quite a riddle, but his vague words took a little time for me to needle out.

I was still being raked with feelings of angst. There was no way around that, since I was submersed in wrath here. But I could control this level of emotion. I just couldn't look at them. Even a glimpse would send me into a spiral...obviously.

"See us!" They were chanting it now, and with every cadence a burst of chilled air struck me.

"Fuck off," I said back in a calm voice.

They silenced.

I wanted to open an eye to see what they were doing, but it wasn't worth the risk.

Instead, I moved in the direction of a wall, bumped into it, and then started following it with as much pace as I could.

"Open your eyes," tempted a void that was clearly close by. "We can free you from your pain."

"The only pain I feel is you idiots. I was just fine until I looked at you."

I sensed hesitation in its movement, but I kept trudging forward. My assumption was that my friendly pursuing dragon contingency was not as easily affected by these things as me. So far I'd made it through, but these creepy things could get me to end myself before the dragons even arrived, if I weren't careful.

One step at a time.

"That hurt, you know?" the void said.

I raised an eyebrow but kept my eyes shut. "Huh?"

"The implication of your words is that you felt pain because you find us unattractive," it replied.

"Yeah," hissed a bunch of others, sending that wonderful blast of cold along.

"We're well aware that we don't have faces, and maybe that's not appealing to the likes of someone like you, but you don't have to be a dick about it."

I stopped.

I frowned.

I turned and opened my eyes.

My hand reached for Boomy.

I slammed my eyes shut again.

"Damn it," I said with a grunt. "Stop doing that shit and I'll talk to you."

"Doing what shit?" the void asked, sounding genuinely perplexed.

"You honestly don't know?" I replied. "How can you not know?"

"What?"

Unbelievable.

"I'm not saying that you guys are ugly," I explained. "It's

just that every time I look at you, my brain starts giving me reasons as to why I should end my own life."

"Oh, that's what you meant?" the void replied in a terse way. "That's our job, man. We're on the level of wrath here, you know?"

"Yes, I know," I said, wondering what the fuck was seriously going on right now. "Look, has it ever occurred to you that maybe people who come through here don't *want* to kill themselves?"

There was a general murmuring that was followed by, "No."

I shivered. "Can you quit it with the cold breezes, please?"

"What cold breezes?"

Another cold breeze hit me.

"Never mind. Fact is that people, in general, don't want to kill themselves. Nothing does." I held up my hand. "Again, that's generally speaking."

The murmuring began again. I couldn't understand anything they were saying since their native language consisted of hisses. It sounded kind of like Morse code, but with a larger communication set than just dashes and dots.

While they were yammering on, I continued on my merry way down the wall.

I cracked open my eyes to see that none of them were in front of me.

There was also no pain.

No anguish.

No suicidal thoughts.

So as long as I wasn't looking *at* one of them, everything was fine? Sweet.

I still felt the general grumpiness associated with this level, but having my eyes open meant I could move more swiftly toward my goal.

I began running as fast as I could, staying near the wall so

I could slow down and shut my eyes when the voids finished their discussion and came after me.

"Wait up," I heard them call out as I got close to the exit. "Please, we beseech you!"

While it was against my better judgment, I stopped just before exiting the area.

They approached.

"Look at us," said the one who had spoken to me earlier. Again, a chill struck me, but it was somewhat diminished. "Please."

"Why?"

"We have discussed your point of view and feel that maybe it is *us* who have been deceived."

This could be useful.

"One sec," I said, stepping toward the stairs and setting Boomy down.

Then I returned, swallowed hard, and opened my eyes.

There was no additional torment.

"Is that better?" they said.

"Yes," I said, noticing that the faceless ones were all unique in some way. Whether it was the shading of their flesh or a slight glow or an angle of their shape, they were all distinguishable. It was somewhat mesmerizing. "Wow."

"What is it?"

"You're all…beautiful," I said, feeling the angst in my mind dissipating.

They glanced at each other and hissed back and forth for a second. Then they nodded at the main void.

He nodded back.

"So, we all want to know…are you being honest when you say that, or are you screwing with us?"

I laughed at that. "I'm being honest. You should look like this all the time."

"We do."

"No," I said, seeking to clarify my meaning, "I'm saying that you should stop with the angry stuff—"

"Wrath," he interrupted. "Not 'angry stuff.' It's wrath. Different thing entirely."

"Right, okay. Well, stop with that, then."

"But we're in the level of wrath," he pointed out again, this time pedantically.

I crossed my arms and glared at him. "And so that means that you all have to exact that wrath? You have no choice? You can't just stand up to the pain like everyone else in the world and choose to be positive?"

"All right, Tony Robbins," said another void, "relax already."

"Shut up, Michelle," said the main one before turning back to me. "Sorry, she can be a bit trying at times."

"Up yours, Keith," she hissed back.

"Anyway," Keith continued, "you were saying that we can choose *not* to be who we are?"

I scrunched my face at him and looked around at all of their…well…faces, I guess.

"Aren't you doing that right now?" I asked pointedly.

More murmurs and then vigorous nods.

"My goodness, we are."

"Feels better than being douchey, doesn't it?" I said.

"Nope."

"Shut up, Michelle," Keith spat over his shoulder. "Yes, it *does* feel better, but our jobs—"

"…Are shitty jobs," I interrupted. "Going through life with the sole purpose of making others want to kill themselves or people around them? What kind of gig is that?" There was no response. "Aren't there things you'd rather be doing with your lives? Do you have no dreams?"

One of the voids raised its hand tentatively.

"Yes?" I said, as they all turned toward it.

"I want to be a poet."

"A poet?" the others replied in unison.

"Yes."

There was quiet for a moment.

"Well, then," said Keith in a supportive voice, "go ahead and recite one of your poems, Estelle."

She put a hand on her chest. "Oh, I couldn't."

The others began coaxing her to share her poetry with them.

"If you're sure you want to hear it, I suppose..." Estelle said finally.

The crowd started chanting, "Poem, poem, poem."

"All right."

Estelle reached into one of her pockets and pulled out a small journal. She thumbed through it for a moment and then cleared her throat.

The sun sends love for flowers
The moon dries tears you cry
The heart soars high like towers
Die Fucker Die

Nobody said a word. They all just stared at Estelle.

"It's called 'Die Fucker Die,'" she said a moment later.

Silence.

"You don't like it?"

Silence.

"I suppose the first few lines could use a little work," Estelle mumbled as she tucked her notebook back into her cloak.

It was clear that everyone was coming to grips with her poetry. I'd heard worse, to be honest, but if everyone in *this* group thought it was messed up, then it was probably pretty messed up.

Another void stepped forward a few moments later. "I've always wanted to be a seamstress."

"Seriously, Jeff?" said Keith.

"You're not one to judge, Keith," Jeff said in an irritated hissing voice. "Just the other day you told me that you wanted to be a ballet dancer."

While Keith had no discernible features, I could tell from his body language that he was in shock. "I told you that in confidence, Jeff."

"Look," I said before things could get out of hand, "it doesn't matter what your dreams are, and it really doesn't matter if people agree with your dreams or not. The point is that you should seek to be happy, as long as you don't do anything that would hurt others...kind of like what you've spent your entire existences doing, if you see what I mean."

"We do," said Keith, rubbing what I assume was his chin. "And you're certain that *all* beings want to live, then?"

"As a general rule, yes," I replied as the sound of voices could be heard across the level. "Uh, that is, everyone except dragons. They despise living, and they're cunning about it. They'll tell you that they want to live, but they don't. So what they do is go out of their way to make others suffer. It helps them deal with things."

The main void tilted his head. "They have done that very thing to us."

"Exactly, Keith," I agreed, pointing at him.

"Then we have only to do our jobs in their presence," he said, nodding slowly. "I understand now."

"Good, good." I licked my lips. "Well, I gotta run. You guys take care of the dragons and then follow your own dreams, yeah?"

Keith moved forward and put his hand out. It was really damn cold, but I shook it.

"We thank you, Nameless One," he said genuinely, his

cold breath freezing my eyebrows. "You have brought us hope in a well of deceit."

"Sure, no problem," I said, grinning. "Good luck, everyone."

As I took off toward the stairs and snapped up Boomy, I heard the voice of Michelle say, "I've always wanted to be a supermodel like the ones we see on Overworld TV when we're allowed to watch."

"Well," Keith said, coughing, "good luck with that."

CHAPTER 25

The feeling of angst disappeared as soon as I got halfway down the stairs.

Wrath was behind me.

I kind of hoped that my discussion with the voids worked, though. It wasn't much of a life for people to spend their days trying to help others do themselves in, after all. Faceless or not, the voids had desires, thoughts, and dreams just like everyone else. No doubt the dragons would seek to screw that up, but that's what bullies did.

Again, though, that was behind me. I was coming to terms with the fact that I was about to face demons.

Ah yes, the level of heresy. Not that the term "heresy" really applied since, again, this wasn't a real hell or anything. Interestingly, though, I *had* felt wrath on the level above. Was that because I had expected to feel it? No, it seemed pretty genuine.

Anyway, what *did* apply was that I'd messed with demons back with that Chippendales-looking dickhead of a mage named Reese. He had used these beasts as batteries to power his takeover of the Overworld. I'd sent the demons packing during that little adventure, and I had a feeling they weren't all that happy about that. In fact, I already knew that they didn't like it that I couldn't be possessed like everyone else. They'd made that abundantly clear when I'd faced them those months ago.

It wasn't like standing here in the shadows was going to get me to the other side, though, so I took a step out and looked around.

You may be under the impression that demons were red or green creatures with horns and pointy teeth, and you'd be right...mostly. Some of them were yellow, blue, pink, and essentially any other shade you could think up. And they were all shapes and sizes, too, which I found interesting. When I saw the demons in the Overworld, they were more wispy until Warren had used his wacky spell on them, but when they changed over they didn't quite look like this. It was kind of throwing me for a loop.

"Well, well, well," said a particularly green medium-sized demon as he walked up to me. "If it isn't good old Officer Ian Dex."

His voice was sinister and there was an angry crease between his eyes.

I shifted uncomfortably.

"What say you hand me that massive weapon of yours and then we take a little walk?"

"Uh...I'm not really into demons."

"Not *that* weapon, Officer Ian Dex," he said, and then tapped on Boomy. "That one."

"Oh, right!" I glanced around and saw a number of interested faces looking our way. I took Boomy out and handed it over. "Be gentle with it."

He squinted at me and then grabbed my elbow and pushed me forward into the mass of demons.

They made a path that seemed fitting for someone who

was headed for the gallows. I was obviously that someone, and that was rather disheartening.

The fact that I was going to be destroyed by the very demons that I cast out of the Overworld was somewhat fitting, though, and I couldn't quite blame them for wanting to get revenge, but I was only doing my job. It wasn't like I just ran about shooting demons for the fun of it. I was a cop; they were tormenting the Vegas Strip. What was I supposed to do?

Looking at all the piercing stares, it seemed to me that this level was more befitting of the term "wrath" than level five. At least at the moment.

"Where are we going?" I said over my shoulder.

"To see our beloved leader."

"Satan?"

The demon laughed. "You read too many books, Officer Ian Dex."

"I really don't," I replied as we kept pushing forward.

The middle of the level was wider than the other circles I'd been in thus far, and this one had a large platform where a gigantic demon sat upon an even bigger throne. Honestly, this dude was massive.

As we got closer to him, I started noticing that demons were whispering my name to each other.

Did everyone get this kind of treatment?

Probably.

A particularly hideous pink-skinned demon winked at me as we walked by.

Ew.

"Halt," said a purple guard who wore rusty armor.

Of all the ones I'd seen thus far, this devil-chick was pretty hot. It probably had to do with the fact that she was dressed for battle…and she was carrying a whip.

Interesting.

"You are Officer Ian Dex," she bellowed, reminding me that the end of my life was near. She then hit me in the gut with the handle side of her whip, dropping me to my knees. "Bow, you fool. You are standing before the queen of the damned, Lucy Für."

It took me a couple of moments to catch my breath.

"You're kidding about that being her name, right?" I said, glancing up at the guard. "And that's a queen?"

Her hand tightened on the whip. I raised my hands in surrender.

"Have him rise," said the queen in a baritone voice. "I will review him now."

I was pulled back to my feet as everyone moved out of the way, leaving me to face the giant demon queen one on one.

CHAPTER 26

"You are Officer Ian Dex," she said without emotion. She held up Boomy. My poor gun was the size of a pin in her hands. "And this is the weapon that you fired at my lovelies, no?"

I glanced around, looking for any of them that may be considered "lovely." There were none. The guard-chick revved my engine, sure, but she sure as hell wasn't "lovely."

"It is," I said finally. "It didn't do much to them, though."

"No, it didn't," she agreed. "But you persisted in sending them back here, yes?"

This felt a lot like those times when I was living with a foster parent and I'd done something really wrong. They'd sit me down and get all adult on me until I finally admitted something. Then they'd ground me for a week and that'd be that. The difference here was that my punishment was more of the eternal type. You know, like eternally dead.

But there was no way out of it.

She knew what I'd done.

"Technically, yes," I said, glancing left and right, "but you must understand that I only did what I had to do in order to protect my town."

Lucy Für leaned back and regarded me.

"I'm listening," she said, setting Boomy on the arm of her chair.

If nothing else, I had a chance to explain the situation. It wasn't likely that it would change the outcome, and it was giving the damn dragons more time to catch up to me—assuming they made it past the voids anyway, but it was worth a shot.

"Right," I said, gathering my memories. "You see, there was this real dick of a mage terrorizing the Strip." I looked up. "His name was Reese."

"We know who he was."

"Yeah, well, then you may recall that he was using some of your demons as batteries."

The faces around me sneered.

"Lovelies," I hastily corrected. "I meant to call them lovelies."

The sneers stayed in place.

"Go on," said Lucy.

I took a deep breath.

"Anyway, it's my job to protect the innocent. Now, I know that this may sound like a foreign concept to you, but to us it's a way of life." I leaned in. "By us, I mean the Las Vegas Paranormal Police Department."

She held up her finger and adjusted in her chair slightly.

"Why is it that you believe we don't understand the concept of protecting the innocent?"

My eyebrows fought to touch each other.

"Because you're demons," I answered as if it were a dumb question.

"And since we're demons we have no concept of right and wrong?"

"Of course you do," I answered quickly. "You just always choose wrong."

The demon who had brought me up the platform stepped in and said, "He reads too many books, my queen. For example, he thought your name was Satan."

Everyone broke out into laughter, including Lucy Für.

She suddenly stopped and so did everyone else.

The level of power she held was immense.

"Officer Ian Dex," Lucy said casually, "I assure you that what you've heard about us is mostly farcical. I will admit that when we are summoned by mages and wizards, it puts us under a spell that compels us to do evil things. We are very strong, as you may have noticed, and our spiritual power is a pool of magical gold, but when we reside in our own land, we are no different than your people are in the Overworld." It was her turn to lean toward me. "In fact, I'd go as far as to say that you humans often make us look like saints."

Deception.

It was the demon way. Everyone knew this. She was just toying with me, trying to get me to fall for her silky words until I was under her spell.

Not gonna happen.

If I was going to die, it would be with my head held high and my brain under my own command.

But I wasn't dumb; I'd play their little game.

"I had no idea," I said, feigning sorrow. "The things we are taught say—"

"I'm aware of what they say," she stated, cutting me off. "Some of them are true, too, but only inasmuch as they're true of you and your people as well."

"Right, okay."

There was a commotion to the right and a team of

demons walked through the crowd, pushing Claire, Wilbur, and Stan in front of them.

"Shit," I said under my breath.

So now I was either going to be killed and eaten by dragons, or I was going to get ripped to shreds by demons… or both. The demon option would at least be faster.

"Dragon Claire," said Lucy, "what brings you to level six?"

All three dragons pointed at me.

"Officer Ian Dex?" Lucy asked, looking confused. "Why are you after him?"

"He was to be our meal," Claire stated, "but he and his band of friends fought against us. The others barricaded themselves in one of the caves and so we came after this one." She eyed me hungrily. "We felt it only right that we at least get some blood from the gift our mother provided. He also tried to have the voids kill us." She looked me over. "I'll admit that was clever."

"Too bad it didn't work."

"Nearly wished it had," noted Wilbur. "There was one of them reading us poetry that was simply horrid."

"Silence, Wilbur," demanded Claire.

Lucy cleared her throat.

"I understand your situation," said the demon queen, crossing her legs in a very human way. "Unfortunately, Officer Ian Dex is currently under my scrutiny for his involvement in an event that included a few of my lovelies."

"We care not about your trivial matters," Stan said, shaking his arm free from the demon who was holding him.

"Uh, Stan," Claire said, turning toward him.

"You are nothing but a peon in the world of dragons," he continued unabated.

I had the feeling that something bad was going to happen, which was fantastic considering it was going to be focused on one of the dragons…for now.

"Stan," Claire tried again, "you may want to—"

"My ancestors pressed your pathetic, ugly race into the ground," Stan declared hotly. "They forced you to live six levels down, and in my estimation, that was not far enough."

Lucy Für rose from her chair.

"Well, Stan," Claire said with a sigh, "it was nice knowing ya."

The demon queen reached out with the speed of lightning, snatching Stan from his defiant position, pulled him to her mouth, and bit his head clean from his body. Then she threw his lower half across the room into a fire that was raging by the far wall.

She sat down and spit Stan's head out.

"Blech," she said with a sour face. "You dragons really taste like shit."

I was beside myself with wonder at what had just happened.

Claire and Wilbur were visibly shaken.

"What's the matter," I whispered to Claire, "are dragons no match for demons or something? Pathetic."

"Stow it, steak dinner," she replied with a whisper of her own. "You'll be on our plate in no time."

"Steak dinner?"

"As I was saying," the queen announced in a dark voice that shut both Claire and me up instantly, "Officer Ian Dex is under my scrutiny at the present time." Her eyes narrowed. "Do either of you wish to challenge that as your brother just did?"

The dragons shook their heads swiftly.

"I didn't think so," Lucy stated. "Now, as for you, Officer Ian Dex, your story—brief as it was—is essentially in line with what was reported to me by my lovelies."

I looked down at my feet.

So this was how it ended. Me getting picked up, having

my head bitten off, and then spat back out because I tasted like shit. What a way to go. Part of me hoped she actually *enjoyed* the taste of my head enough to just chomp me down completely. That would at least be a little jab at the dragons to show them that humans tasted better than they did.

It was stupid, I knew, but I was facing my doom here.

"You have done us a great service, Officer Ian Dex," she said in such a way that was oddly warm and caring.

I blinked. "Huh?"

"By releasing my lovelies from the mage's grip, they were able to return home and be with their families again."

"No shit?" I said, perplexed.

"Ask of us that which you desire and we shall grant it to you." She held up a finger. "Think carefully, though, for you only get one wish of us."

My first thought was to have them kill these other two dragons, and the look on Claire's face told me that she assumed I was going to do just that.

But these were *demons* I was dealing with here. If I asked her to kill the dragons, where would that leave me? Besides, the chances were very good that she was going to kill them anyway. At least if her actions against Stan were any indication.

"I'd ask simply for safe passage to level seven, ma'am," I said finally.

There was a collective groan.

I looked around, wincing. "Did I say something wrong?"

Lucy Für stood up and handed Boomy to me. Her hand was ginormous.

"They were hoping you were going to ask us to kill the dragons," she answered, "which would have been great because we are only allowed to kill them under three circumstances: they attack us, a worthy soul requests us to kill them, or they insult us." She said that last bit while pointing at the head of Stan.

"Oh, sorry, everyone," I said. "I just figured that if I asked for that, you'd all have killed the dragons and then ripped me to shreds, too."

"We would have," Lucy said matter-of-factly. "That's the other reason they're upset."

"Ah."

Lucy glanced at her flock.

"But we are honorable in our dealings, Officer Ian Dex. You will find safe passage to level seven, and then we will let the dragons resume their hunt." She then tilted her head at Claire. "Unless you'd like to argue the point, dragon?"

She didn't.

CHAPTER 27

*T*he demons were true to their word. I got all the way to the stairs and halfway down before I heard Lucy yell, "Release the dragons!"

At least there were only two of them left. Not that I could defeat two dragons, or likely even one, but it was certainly easier than defeating three. Actually, come to think of it, I'd probably have had a better chance at three because I could play them off each other. Then again, I'd still end up wasting one and be back to two, making it the same situation I was in now.

Either way, that was neither here nor there at this point.

"Two is the number and the number shall be two," I said in paraphrase of a Monty Python line.

Level seven was the area for valkyries, those lovely chicks who decided those who may die in battle and those who may live. In Dante's world, this was the level of violence. Seeing that the valkyries did the life/death choosing thing, it seemed like a fitting place for them.

But did that mean there were battles constantly going on down here?

147

I listened for the sounds of violence.

Nothing.

I poked my head out and glanced around. No swordplay, no guns, no cannons, no wrestling matches…nothing.

The sound of footsteps clomped down the stairs, signaling that Claire and Wilbur were hot on my trail.

"Time to go," I said, taking a brisk step through the entrance to level seven. "Just walk fast and get through this damn thing."

I got a quarter of the way to the other side when I heard Claire call out.

"Stop, this instant."

I gave her the finger and started running.

If I had been just your average, every-day human, they would have caught up to me in no time. But I'm *not* an average human, which meant I kept well ahead of them.

Unfortunately, I didn't realize that this section had a pit.

Yes, a pit.

It was a large arena-type area that was covered with dirt.

I knew this because I had run right over an edge that was cleverly disguised. In fact, I hadn't seen it until the moment I was falling toward the ground.

It hurt.

With a groan, I pushed myself up and walked toward the center of the arena, looking around to weigh the situation.

If I were a betting man, which I was, I would have claimed that I was standing in a place rather similar to a Roman gladiator field. I tried to see if there were bleachers of some sort, but nothing was visible. The area that would have been where the crowd was, happened to be completely black. I didn't mean dark—I could see fine in the dark. I meant black, like it was blocked off somehow.

"Hello?" I said, thinking that Claire and Wilbur would be dropping in at any moment. Literally. "Anyone there?"

The darkness lifted slightly, revealing a crowd of about one hundred, all seated in a horseshoe-shaped set of bleachers.

I waved sheepishly, not knowing what else to do.

A flash off to my right caused me to jump.

She was a seven-foot tall, musclebound blonde with amber eyes that sparkled, and perfect teeth. Her face was triangular and it was marked with black lines that had been expertly painted.

Drool.

"You are in the land of the valkyries," she said in a voice that matched her mystique.

"Yeah, I know," I replied, thinking that now might be the time to take out Boomy…or the Admiral.

"Who are Boomy and the Admiral?" said the Amazonian love goddess. "And I am not a love goddess."

"Oh, sorry."

I'd have to control what I was thinking, obviously. She was just so damn hot!

"Thank you," she said sincerely. "Now, who are Boomy and the Admiral? It sounds like a comedy team."

"Oh, uh, Boomy is my gun," I said, stammering, "and the Admiral is my…uh…well, my junk."

"Your junk?" Her eyes creased and she studied me. "Do you mean your manhood?"

I coughed. "Yeah."

"I see." The valkyrie blew out a long breath, looking somewhat disappointedly at me. "What is your name?"

"Ian," I answered. "Ian Dex. And yours?"

"Valerie," she answered.

"Valerie the valkyrie?"

"Correct." She took two steps forward. "Ian Dex, do you hold a position of power where you are from?"

I blinked at her while feeling somewhat taken aback by her question.

"Yeah," I said in a drawn out way.

"And have you held this position for very long?"

"Five years," I answered. "What's your point?"

She was nodding as she began circling me.

I had the feeling that the dragons should have been here by now. Actually, they should have arrived a while ago.

"They are frozen in time," Valerie stated. "I shall release them once I'm finished speaking with you."

"Actually," I said with a bit of hopefulness, "you may feel free to keep them suspended for as long as you'd like."

She paused and looked me in the eye.

Melt.

"You had thought to show us your gun and then your... junk, as you put it?"

"Really only the gun," I said. "The 'junk' part of my thinking wasn't actually going to happen. I just—"

"Many men who come into power..." She paused as a juvenile thought struck regarding her sentence. She then gave me a sharp look. "Do you turn *everything* into innuendo?"

"Sorry," I replied with a grimace. "I can't help it."

I had to clear my thoughts.

Obviously she could read my mind, so if everything was blank or at least pointless—which Rachel would have argued was the case—I could at least build time to get out of this level and on to the next.

Daisies were the first thing to come to mind. I don't know why, but my guess was that they were innocuous. What could possibly go wrong thinking about Daisies? The image of Daisy Wilson came to mind. She was one of my college sweethearts. Great ass, better rack. There were days where I could have spent hours playing "Hide the Admiral" with her.

"Honestly, Ian Dex," Valerie said with a disgusted look, "you are perverse."

"I know that," I retaliated. "It's in my genetic makeup, and the enhancements I was given by the PPD only make it worse."

"Yes," she said. "You are a cop."

"That's right."

"It's an interesting point."

Was that interesting bad or interesting good? I couldn't tell by the look on her face.

"Interesting neutral," she replied.

I put my hands on my hips. "Will you stop reading my mind, please? It's rude."

That seemed to shock her.

"It is?"

"Of course it is. What's in my head is between me and… well, me. You have no right to be poking around in my thoughts."

"But your thoughts define you."

"They do not," I challenged. "My thoughts mostly surface unintentionally. What defines me, or anyone, is what is done with those thoughts."

"You mean your actions?"

I nodded in response.

"Interesting."

"Not really," I said, relaxing slightly. "If I followed through with every thought I ever had, I'd be serving time. Asshole drivers alone would put me behind bars for years, especially those fuckers who have fancy cars so they feel it's their right to take up two spaces. Douchebags."

She seemed to be considering my words.

"Either way," she said, "your thoughts regarding the showing of your 'junk' to me—or to anyone without their express request—is unwelcome, regardless of what you may think."

"I know that, lady," I spat back, "and I'd *never* do anything like that in reality. I'm not a comedian or a news anchor."

"But your thoughts—"

"Again, they don't define me. What does is how I react to my thoughts. You hear no filter because you're in my head, which, again, is rude. But did you see me actually whip out the Admiral and start flapping him around? No, you didn't."

By now I was pretty heated. Yeah, I knew I was a seriously horny dude, although today's events were enough to scare the sex right out of me. But I wasn't a degenerate. My perversions were sequestered to the bedroom, behind closed doors, and only with willing participants.

"That's good," she said. Then she winced. "Sorry, I read your thoughts again."

"I noticed."

"It's what we do."

"Yeah, about that… Are you going to let me go or what?"

Valerie snapped her fingers and the two dragons fell to the ground with a thud. They both jumped to their feet swiftly, clearly able to handle the fall better than I had.

Showoffs.

"I am Claire," announced Claire as she walked toward Valerie. "I am heir to the throne of—"

"I know who you are," Valerie interrupted. "And I know that your brother is named Wilbur." She tilted her head. "Stan has died?"

"Demons," I said before Claire could respond.

"Ah. Yes, they do that sort of thing."

Claire continued walking forward, the resolve on her face apparent. She was going to play the power-card here. I had a feeling that was a bad idea.

"And your feeling, Ian Dex, would be correct," said Valerie. And then, "Sorry."

"What are you talking about?"

"Dragon Claire," Valerie stated, turning away from me, "you are chasing Ian Dex in order to dine on his flesh, but you are in the land of valkyries now. The only way we can allow this is for you to do battle in the ring. Whoever wins shall be awarded life."

"Fine with me," said Claire with a wry grin.

"Not me," I argued. "If I recall correctly, Valerie, valkyries require duels to be of the equitable kind, no?"

"Of course."

"And do you honestly think that I have even the slightest chance of beating a dragon in a fight?"

Valerie glanced in my general direction and said, "Hmmm, you may be correct."

"Exactly."

"But I know of one thing in which you are compatible with dragons, Ian Dex."

I couldn't think of one. Claire could blow fire; I couldn't. Wilbur could turn into a gigantic, flying beast; I couldn't. They could both armor themselves with rows of scales, even when in human form; I couldn't. I *could* run as fast as them, but that wasn't likely the competition that a valkyrie wanted to witness.

"No," agreed Valerie. "That's not it." She winced. "Oh, again, sorry."

"So what are you talking about?" I asked.

She turned and began walking toward the bleachers.

"Sexuality."

The two dragons and I all said, "What?"

CHAPTER 28

"Come again?" I said.

"Have you already done so once?" said Valerie as she took the chair that sat at the base of the bleachers. It clearly marked her as the leader of the valkyries. "That was certainly faster than I'd expected."

"No, I don't mean that," I replied sourly. "And you say *I* take everything as innuendo?"

She adjusted uncomfortably in her chair while glancing around at her subjects.

"Anyway," I said, "what is it you want us to do exactly?"

"It's not that hard, Ian Dex," she answered and then gave me a quick look. I *hadn't* thought of anything naughty, so I gave her an accusing look back. She coughed and then continued. "As you pointed out, it's no contest for you to fight these two, and we have an agreement that dragons do not have to fight each other when coming through this area. But we also cannot allow you, Ian Dex, to pass through our level without a battle of some sort."

I scanned the bleachers and noted that all of the valkyries were just as hot as Valerie. If this had been the naughty level

JOHN P. LOGSDON & CHRISTOPHER P. YOUNG

instead of the violent one, I could see myself living here. It'd be heaven for a guy like me.

"Thank you," the crowd said in unison.

I nearly fell down at the power of their voices.

"Stop reading Ian Dex's thoughts," commanded Valerie. "He finds it intrusive."

"Thank you."

"No worries." Valerie stood again and put her hands out. "Now, since you cannot hope to survive battle against these two, you will instead compete in the realm of sexuality."

The three of us looked at each other uncomfortably. Well, at least Claire and I shared a sour look. Wilbur was pursing his lips slightly while wiggling his eyebrows in my direction.

He winked.

"Ew," I said, unable to control my reaction.

I started walking toward Valerie with purpose. In response, the entirety of the valkyries stood up and brandished their swords. At that, I started walking *away* from Valerie with purpose.

My hands were up.

"Okay, okay," I said. "Jeez. I was just going to talk to her. You babes are touchy."

They resumed their seated positions.

"What exactly do you mean by sexuality, Val?" I asked after my adrenaline got under control. "Like a striptease or something?"

"Oooh," the crowd said with much enthusiasm.

"Silence," Valerie ordered. The valkyries complied without hesitation. "That would be an unfair test for the dragons. Much like you can't compete with them in battle, they could not compete with you in pole dancing."

Obviously she could not only read my active thoughts, Valerie also had some way of getting intel on my history. It was true that I was well-versed in pole dancing. I wasn't a

Chippendales dancer or anything, but I'd dated a number of pole dancers in my day, so I'd had a pole installed in my condo. I'd watched and learned. Chicks seemed to dig it when I'd added the pole dancing to my own sensual disrobing, so I'd brushed up until perfecting the skill.

"Then what do you mean?" Claire asked, standing defiantly.

"That you all have sex with each other," Valerie stated in such a way that signaled she believed this was a perfectly fine thing to demand. "The one who is least performant in our eyes, will be the one who loses their life."

Claire grunted and shook her head. "Uh, no way I'm screwing my brother."

Wilbur shook his head in disgust, clearly in line with his sister's thinking.

"Yeah, that's gross," I agreed. "You can't have these two bone each other. It's just nasty. Oh, and I'm not screwing him either."

Wilbur pouted.

The valkyries went silent and their eyes all closed. There were nods, shakes of heads, tilts of heads, and so on. They were clearly discussing the situation telepathically. Kind of like how the PPD team could by employing the connector, but obviously they had no need for such a device.

Finally, they opened their eyes.

"We have decided," announced Valerie. "Claire and Wilbur will not be required to participate with each other as we understand the taboo involved in such action."

Wilbur and Claire looked relieved. I was, too. That would have been just wrong.

"However, you will be required to perform with both of them individually, Ian Dex."

"Just kill me, then," I said.

"What?" the valkyries chorused.

"I'm not boning a dude," I replied with a shrug. "That's just as taboo to me as these two knocking bottoms with each other."

They seemed confused by my statement, and Wilbur was clearly unhappy.

"Look, I'm all about people doing what they want and such, and I don't hold any prejudice against a person's sexual preference, but I'm not gay and I'm not going to bone a dude just to satisfy your weird fantasies."

The valkyries all glanced back and forth at each other. I'd clearly touched a nerve.

"Don't go playing the 'shocked' game, ladies," I said, wagging my finger at them. "I know full well what's going on here. I'm a horndog, remember?" They studied their feet. "Yeah, I know you knew that about me because you can read my mind and you obviously know a lot more than just my active thoughts. You all want a show. You want to see me in action."

Their innocent looks turned more to agreeable looks.

"Exactly." I sniffed. "I'd be more than happy to bone any—or *all*—of you, but I'm not boning Wilbur." I shrugged at him. "No offense, man. I'm just not into dudes."

He sighed. "Haven't you ever heard the saying, 'Once you go gay, you stay that way?'"

"Uh, no," I replied. "And I don't think it works like that, Wilbur."

I *had* created my own little saying once that went, "Once you go amalgamite, you come back every night."

The valkyries giggled, revealing that they were still reading my thoughts.

I gave them an "oh, come on!" look.

They studied their shoes again.

"Look, Val," I said after a few seconds, "if you want to kill me, go ahead...but, again, I'm not boning a dude."

Their eyes closed again and they all smiled while nodding.

"We have decided," Valerie said with a twinkle in her eye.

She snapped her fingers and Wilbur disappeared. Both Claire and I looked around the arena, but he was nowhere to be found.

"Have you killed my brother?" Claire said, sounding almost hopeful.

Dragons were a warped bunch.

"We have not," Valerie stated. "Seeing that he has a particular interest in things that are not shared by Ian Dex, but also noting that he must perform as you must, I contacted our friends on level two and made an arrangement with them."

"The satyrs?" I said.

"Exactly. They are more than willing to work with his interests and report back their honest assessment of his participation."

I wanted to say "ew" again, but I was too grossed out to bother.

"He's probably having the time of his life," Claire whispered. "He wrote in his diary that he's been dying to visit that level for a little extracurricular activity."

"Ew." I couldn't resist that time. "Wait, you read his diary?"

"Sure, why not?"

"Because it's personal," I said as if that were a dumb question.

Claire shrugged and then held her hand up high. "Could we have a moment without all of you listening to our thoughts and discussion? It is in the dragon/valkyrie agreement."

Valerie nodded and the crowd's eyes all closed.

"What are you doing?" I said, knowing full well that Claire was up to something.

"We're going to have to bone each other," she said. "It's the only way."

I gave her the once over. "Seriously?"

Don't get me wrong here. Claire was incredibly hot in her humanoid form, but she was also looking to kill me. That didn't exactly put my libido into overdrive. I was all about a little rough play, sure, but Claire's was the kind that didn't give the option for a safe word.

"If we don't, they'll kill us both," she replied with a shrug. "And if we don't put on one hell of a show, they'll kill one of us, because I can guarantee that Wilbur is going to go all out with those satyrs."

I didn't want to think about Wilbur's situation. That would definitely *not* help matters in my nether region.

"Well," I said as I rubbed my chin, "I guess it would give an entire new meaning to you eating me."

CHAPTER 29

*S*o, anyway, *that* happened.

While I'm not going to go into details, I'll just say that it was definitely the best performance of my life, and I'd go even further to state that Claire was beyond amazing in the sack.

We were both woozy as we stood before the valkyries.

They, in turn, were all swooning.

Claire and I could have seriously hit it off under different circumstances. Dating a dragon was, again, too dicey to entertain, but…yeah. I gave her another onceover. Shame.

"Well?" she said in a tired voice. "What's the verdict?"

"We have a draw," Valerie replied.

"A three-way?" I said, and then held up my hand at seeing that sparkle in Valerie's eyes. "I don't mean that in a sexual way, Val. I'm asking you if we have a three-way draw, meaning that me, Claire, and Wilbur are all tied up with each other?" I groaned again. "And I don't mean 'tied up' like that, either."

Honestly, these chicks needed to get laid. I'd be happy to

be the guy who came down for regular visits to help them out, too, but only if specific rules were set in place.

All of their eyes were sparkling now.

"Still reading my thoughts, I see," I said with an accusing stare. "Well, note that I'm serious about what I just thought, but that's not going to happen if I lose this little tournament of yours, and as far as I remember, you *must* choose a loser, no?"

Valerie snapped her fingers.

"What happened?" I said.

"Wilbur lost," she replied.

"Yes," Claire said with a fist-pump.

I gave her a disturbed look. "Seriously? He's your brother!"

"Less competition," she replied with a shrug.

Dragons were a fucked-up bunch, which only went to show that I wasn't going to even entertain dating Claire. I kind of felt bad about having boned her, in fact. Oh well, at least I'd been on top for most of it.

"Fine," I said, giving up on understanding the nuances of dragon culture. "Now what happens?"

"We will hold Dragon Claire here until you proceed through level eight," Valerie replied.

Claire put her hands on her hips. "You can't do that!"

"There is no precept in our dealings with dragons that precludes us from detaining you for as long as we wish, Dragon Claire. We are only giving Ian Dex an advantage because…" She paused and adjusted again in her chair. "Well, we have our reasons."

Claire's mouth hung open.

"Son of a bitch," she said as she slowly turned toward me. "You've made a deal with them to come back and bone them, haven't you?"

"More of an agreement," I admitted, "but it's a win-win as

far as I'm concerned."

Sparkling eyes all around. They were definitely going to be a fun bunch to enjoy.

Their heads nodded in agreement.

"I don't suppose you could just snap your fingers and send me to the end of level nine, Val?"

"Sorry, no," she replied. "We could only do that with Wilbur because he was part of our contest, and because the satyrs allowed for it."

"Swell. So that means that I need to get past the fae on my own."

"I'm afraid that's true," Valerie stated. "They can be rather tricky, too, so we ask that you tread carefully."

She stepped down and walked over to me. Even though I'd just finished an epic session of hide-the-sausage with Claire, I felt quite capable of playing a round or two with Valerie. She was just smokin' hot.

"You're sweet," she said.

I frowned. "All right, it's going to have to be in the contract that you *can't* read my thoughts."

She wore a sad face.

"Trust me," I said, looking up into those glittering eyes, "if you *don't* know what I'm thinking, the surprise of the things I do will only serve to improve the experience."

Her sad face disappeared.

She nodded and then bent down to hug me. It was a little awkward because she was huge, but even more strange was that she'd grabbed my buttocks and gave them a squeeze.

It burned.

"Ouch," I said, pulling away. "What the hell was that?"

"You are now marked as being allowed to enter the seventh level once," she replied with an evil grin. "When you wish to do so, merely recite the phrase, 'I want me some

163

valkyrie lovin'" and you'll immediately appear in a safe zone of our arena."

I wasn't sure how to reply to that.

"Finish your mission," she said, placing her hand on my shoulder. "If you survive, say the statement and we will formalize our contract and give you a permanent means to move freely between your world and our level whenever you wish."

I laughed. "Sounds perfect."

"It will be."

I nodded and smiled at Claire. She did not share my enthusiasm. In fact, she appeared downright pissed off.

That made me even happier.

"Any suggestions on how I can get past the fae?" I asked her.

"You want *my* help?" Claire answered with a shocked laugh.

"If they kill me, you lose your prize."

"Shit, you're right." Her shoulders slumped. "Hit them with a riddle. Make them take you across before you'll answer it." Her eyes trained on me. "And it'd better be a good one or you're screwed."

"Right," I said with a nod. "Thank you."

"Fuck you."

I raised a mischievous eyebrow at her. "I thought you'd be too tired to go again so soon."

The eyes in the crowd sparkled.

CHAPTER 30

I didn't even bother to hesitate this time around. I knew exactly what to do and I was already well aware of what fae looked like. They looked like super-attractive humans.

So I strode out into the level and headed directly for the other side.

This caught them off guard.

It was quite amazing what people will let you get away with by simply acting like you know what the hell you were doing. In fact, I got to nearly the halfway point until a bunch of fae moved to block my continued progress.

"Halt," said a tall dude with wavy brown hair. He was tan, smooth-skinned, and had green eyes. Wilbur—rest his…well, whatever it was that dragons had—would have approved. "What do you think you're doing?"

"I'm walking toward the exit over there so that I can get to level nine," I replied, then I waved my hand dismissively at him. "If you'll excuse me, I have a timetable to keep."

A few of them moved, but the big guy did not.

"You can't just walk into our level and pass through. That's not how it works."

"Ah, yes," I said, snapping my fingers. "I remember now. You are the ones who like dealing in riddles." Their faces lit up. "You will attempt to use them on me until I falter. If I fail to answer any of the ever-increasingly difficult mental puzzles you throw my way, then my life shall be forfeit." I paced in front of the fae wall. "However, if I succeed in deciphering each volley you deliver, by the time I get to the other side, then I may walk through the exit unscathed."

Their faces were now holding looks of surprise.

The big dude nodded at me. "You're obviously well-read. I would not have expected this from a vampire."

"Why does everyone keep saying that?" I said, irritated.

"Because you're obviously good-looking, you have chiseled features, you have—"

"No, I mean about my being well-read." My eye felt like it was twitching. That gave me pause. Was I more irritated about people thinking I was a vampire or about them thinking I was somehow scholarly? And why would I be upset about people thinking me smart? "Anyway, I'm *not* a vampire and I also don't read good."

"Well."

"Well what?"

"You don't read well," the big dude stated.

I stared at him dully. "I know, I just said that. No point in rubbing it in."

He furrowed his brow at me and let out a slow breath through his nose.

"Right, well, you are correct in your assessment," he said. "We must therefore begin our questioning of you immediately since you have already managed to cover half the distance unimpeded."

I was expecting this, but what they weren't expecting was

that Claire had given me a tidbit of information to counter them. While it wasn't in their rules to decipher riddles I posed, Claire's words made it clear that they would comply.

"Before you begin," I said, rubbing my hands together, "I'll bet that I know of a riddle that *you* will not be able to solve."

They laughed and shook their heads at me. It almost felt like they considered me a child. This was rather rude, but I just held a stoic and somewhat pompous gaze at them all.

The big dude gained his composure first. "Wait, are you being serious?"

"Deadly," I replied.

That squelched their chuckling.

I'd thrown down the gauntlet.

The big dude had a look on his face that told me he had no choice but to accept my challenge. This clearly bothered him, but I didn't care. My life was more important to me than his pride.

"Well, then," he said in a measured tone of voice, "what is this riddle you claim I cannot solve?"

"Walk with me and I shall tell you," I stated as I began my stride right toward the fae wall.

To my surprise, it opened up and I was soon making steps toward the exit with the big dude by my side.

"Okay," I said in a voice loud enough to be heard for a good distance, "what has eleven legs, is purple, and can sing opera when it goes up a hill, but has thirteen legs, is green, and cannot sing opera when it comes back down the hill?"

There was no immediate response, which was fully expected.

"So," said the big dude, "it has eleven legs going up the hill and thirteen coming back down?"

"Yes."

"And it is purple when going up, but green when coming back down?"

"Correct."

"And it can sing opera on the way up but not on the way down?"

"You've got it."

The walk was nearly silent aside from the clomping of shoes on the hard floor. Every face within visual range was deep in thought. Their eyes were bouncing all over the place, signaling that I had most certainly given them a puzzle that was sinisterly complex.

I was completely shocked when we got all the way to the opposite side of the level and there hadn't been a single word spoken.

They all stopped twenty feet away from the exit. I went all the way up to it and turned around, standing within jumping distance of the stairs, just in case.

"Well," I said, smiling, "here we are. Do you have an answer for me?"

If you've never seen a bunch of defeated-looking fae, you haven't lived. They were notoriously snobbish and better-than-thou in their dealings. To see them standing before me wearing faces of inferiority was immensely rewarding.

"No," admitted the big dude. "Tell us, what is this thing that has eleven legs, is purple, and can sing opera when it goes up the hill, but has thirteen legs, is green, and cannot sing opera when it comes back down?"

I grinned and turned away, facing the stairs.

"I have no idea," I called over my shoulder, and then ran like hell.

CHAPTER 31

*F*ae typically didn't use a ton of foul language, but the ones who were halfway down the stairs behind me sounded like drunken sailors. These guys were unrolling a stream of obscenities so vile that it could have been used for inspiration for one of Estelle's poems.

But that was level eight, and it was now behind me.

Level nine was my new problem, and I *still* could not remember who was down here.

My first thought was Satan, but the demons would have laughed at that.

One thing was for certain, whatever it was on level nine, there was only one of them. I knew this because the instructors had drilled it into our heads during training. They said that the…whatever it was, was not something to be trifled with. Now, considering all the levels I'd just been through, I can't imagine anything above that *was* trifle-worthy, so the creature on level nine had to be pretty dire indeed.

I stepped out and glanced around.

This level was nice. I'm talking Las Vegas five-star-hotel nice.

Where the other levels had rock floors or were covered with goop or satyr essence, this circle of "hell" had polished marble. The walls were clean and sleek, covered with paintings so vivid and beautiful that it threatened to take my breath away. Even Warren's rune paintings paled in comparison, and those had been quite something. There were couches, chairs, tapestries, tables, and pretty much everything you would expect in one of the most luxurious lobbies in the best of hotels on the Strip.

The question I had was: Who was this all for?

Me?

"Hello," said a voice so smooth that the hairs on my neck stood up. It was practiced, flawless, and warm. Very warm. "Allow me to welcome you to the ninth level."

I turned and saw a man wearing a black suit that was fitted perfectly. He was built roughly the same as me, though the V-shape that went from his shoulders to his waist was less pronounced. His hair was black and slicked back, which looked quite chic. His smile was dazzling. I mean seriously dazzling. And it was so genuine that I found myself smiling back almost instantly. Truth was that I should have felt freaked out and on my toes, but I wasn't. I was calm, cool, and relaxed. This was doubly strange since I couldn't see his eyes. He was wearing dark sunglasses. Considering the lighting in the area was rather dim, I couldn't understand why he'd need shades, and it made me think he was hiding something, but...I didn't care.

Something in the back of my head told me that the fact that I didn't care should be worrying me.

"You are Officer Ian Dex, right?" he asked.

"Just call me Ian," I replied, reaching out my hand, though I didn't know why.

He shook my hand. His grip was firm and warm.

"My name is Basil," he said.

At least it wasn't Lucifer, which I found humorous as I recalled the demon queen's name from level six.

"What brings you to level nine, Ian?"

"Same old story," I said, waving my hand. "A bunch of cops get tricked by a dragon, who sends her kids to eat us, we get separated, the dragons chase me through the nine levels, and I try to get to the other side before being gooped on, fucked to death, eaten, killed, and all those other lovely things that come with the various circles." I shrugged. "I just want to get to my crew."

"I see," he said with a slow nod. "So you're not on some quest of fealty or some kind of learning event?"

"Oh, no, nothing like that. I'm the chief of the Las Vegas Paranormal Police Department. My crew is on the other side of the tunnel that connects through here. I'm just trying to get to them."

"Hmmm." He smiled again. "That sounds innocuous enough."

"That's what I thought," I replied, leaning in conspiratorially. This guy was making me feel more comfortable than I should have. "But it turns out that everyone on the various levels wants your...well, whatever they each want, regardless of what *you* want."

"It's their way," he said. "You can't blame a beast for acting in accordance with its instinct. A lion does not attack the elk because there is hate in its heart or because of some political agenda. It does so merely because the lion is a predator and the elk is its prey."

I grimaced. "Still sucks to watch it."

He smiled again. This time it didn't feel as pleasant. This time it felt devilish.

Were there other names for Satan that I didn't know

about? There were a few I *did* know, like Abaddon and Apollyon. I glanced his way. Could Basil be short for Beelzebub? Or maybe Belial?

"Come along, Ian," he said as he turned and walked away. I felt compelled to comply. "I shall walk you to the tunnel that you seek."

"Really?" I said, following him.

"Of course. Your purpose is true. Therefore, I will lend aid where I can."

This was odd.

"Well…thanks."

"This surprises you?" he said, glancing over at me.

"If you'd just been through what I've been through over the other eight levels, you'd understand why I'm not exactly feeling all that trusting."

His laugh was the kind that made you feel something bad was about to happen.

Good-looking or not, this dude was creeping me out.

"I understand your trepidation," he said after a moment, "but don't blame them for their atrocities. Again, they are but lions among the elk. You and I, we are thinking men. We do not resort to mere instinct. We rationalize, seeking truth and understanding before coming to our conclusions." He stopped and turned to face me. "We choose when to attack and when to let live."

A pit in my stomach formed at his words.

I'd have to play the game with this guy, too. I didn't know who the hell he was, but everyone and their mother in the academy taught that this was one bad dude. He was clever, yes, but he was also the embodiment of evil.

The side of his mouth turned up in a half-smile that suggested he may be able to hear my thoughts just like the valkyries.

To verify, I turned my mind back to Claire.

"The dragon who follows you is the lion," he declared an instant before resuming our walk. "A wonderful, beautiful lion." He released a serene sigh. "Well, she seems clever enough when in discussion, but her base impulse is to attack. That, of course, makes you the elk, I'm afraid."

"So I gathered," I said as we began heading down an escalator. "Where does this lead?"

"To the lava streams," he answered. "Don't worry, though, I shall deliver you safely to the other side, for you are giving me something that I dearly desire."

"I am?"

"You are," he affirmed.

"What's that?"

He merely smiled again in response.

CHAPTER 32

*B*asil stayed relatively quiet as we traversed the rocks that led us through the pits of lava.

He seemed to be focused on the task at hand, so I didn't want to interrupt his train of thought. I feared if I pestered him in any way, it could make him slip into the pool of fire, and while he may be equipped to survive such a thing, I was relatively certain I could not. Not that I would necessarily fall in after him, but I didn't know how all of this worked, so why chance it? And even if I didn't fall in after him, it may serve to piss him off enough to pull me in anyway.

The interesting part of this journey through this section was that it wasn't hot.

It should have been.

We were surrounded by bubbling, molten rock. That shit was known for being hot and steamy.

But I noticed no change in temperature. In fact, it was almost as if we were walking on a glass-like material that hovered over the burning sea.

I went to test this theory, when Basil said, "I wouldn't do that, if I were you."

Instead of dipping my shoe in the lava, I set it back on the rock and continued following him along. Okay, so lava that doesn't radiate heat exists on level nine. Clearly it was still dangerous stuff or Basil wouldn't have said anything, and it was also apparent that he was a man—or whatever—of his word, since he stopped me from injuring myself.

But I still didn't know what this mysterious thing I was apparently providing to him was, or why he was so happy to receive it.

If it was my "soul" or whatever, why would he go through all this trouble to bring me to the other side of the level before taking it? It was pretty apparent that he could manipulate me quite easily.

This guy had to be the devil, right?

Who else could make you feel equally safe and seriously freaked out in the same instant? The master manipulator, yeah? To be fair, I didn't believe the devil even existed. Yes, I knew all about gods and angels and demons and such, but a single God with a big "G" and a dude who was thrown down into a pit of fire and all that? None of the supernaturals believed that stuff. That was for normals to dig into, not us.

I looked around at the pit of fire and then up at the back of Basil's perfectly slicked-back hair.

"Hmmm," I said with a raised eyebrow. Then I snorted. "Nah."

"You're correct," Basil stated. "I'm not the devil. In fact, there is no devil. Nor is there, as you put it, a God with a big 'G.'" He chuckled. "Clever way to say it, though."

"Thanks." I jumped to another rock. "So who are you, then?"

"I'm Basil," he replied. "We've already been through that."

"I know the name you've given me, but who *are* you?"

He stepped off the rock path and up to a section of the

circle that had a big red "Exit" sign hanging in the air. That was a little awkward.

In response to my question, he removed his glasses and stared into my eyes.

His eyes were swirling pools of yellow that were spinning in opposing directions in a rhythmically hypnotic way.

"Wow," I said. "That's cool."

He jolted upright and tilted his head at me.

"That's odd." He pulled out a mirror and looked at himself. "They seem to be working just fine. Let me try that again."

He tucked the mirror away and then gave me a full stare.

I leaned in and studied his irises. They looked really sweet. I didn't know if this was some kind of magic or a newfangled style of contact lenses, but they were awesome.

"Dude, those things are fantastic."

Basil glanced away. "What the shit is going on?"

"With what?" I asked, confused.

"You should be dead."

"I should?" I then touched my chest and stomach. "I'm not, right?"

He frowned at me. "No, you idiot."

"Name-calling?"

"Sorry," he said with a heavy sigh. "I just don't understand it. I've stared at you. You've looked right into my eyes. Yet, you remain alive."

"So?"

"So I'm a basilisk!"

I snapped my fingers and pointed at him.

"*That's* the name I couldn't remember. Man, it's been driving me nuts. I knew I'd heard it time and again because the teachers really drove it home with us, you know? They were like, beware of the basilisk in level nine because he'll—"

I paused and looked up at him. "Wait, you were going to kill me just now?"

"Duh."

"What the fuck, dude?" I said, putting my hands on my hips. "You said you were going to deliver me safely."

"Over the lava pit, yes," he replied, nodding. "And if you look behind you, you'll see that I've done just that. But I wasn't going to just let you leave."

That was disheartening. Here I was thinking this was some kind of cool guy. Creepy as fuck, sure, but still cool. The hair, the look, the shades...it all rang "mojo."

But...

"You're a dick, man," I said, shoving him in the chest.

His swirly eyes opened very wide.

"Did you just push me?"

"Fucking right, I did," I said as I took a step toward him. "I oughta kick your ass right here and now."

He held up his hands to protect himself.

There may have even been some whimpering going on.

I blinked.

"You're kidding me," I said as I lowered my fists. "You're a wuss?"

"No," he yelled in a pathetic voice.

"Oh, my God," I cackled. "You're a frickin' wuss."

"Don't talk about me like that!"

I crossed my arms. "Or you'll do what?"

"I...I..." He started sobbing.

"Ah jeez," I said, laughing. "This is unbelievable. So you're basically a badass as long as your freaky eye trick works, but if it doesn't, you're just a pussy."

"I..."

He couldn't finish his sentence.

"All right, all right," I said, hesitantly patting him on the shoulder. "Let it all out."

Boy did he.

Basil must have cried for five minutes straight. There were so many tears that wisps of steam *did* come up when the water from his eyes reached the lava pit.

I didn't know whether to feel sorry for him or to berate the hell out of him. Fact was that this dude had probably killed tons of people over the years with his creepy stare. He was finally getting a taste of his own medicine.

Good.

"All right, Basil," I said, lifting up his chin. "I'm not going to kick your ass, but I hope you've learned a lesson here."

"What?"

"How you're feeling right now is probably how everyone you've ever done the freaky eye-swirl thing to felt moments before they died." I shook my head at him. "You should be ashamed."

"I am," he said as his eyes watered again. "I really, really am."

I held up my hand to calm him down. He sniffed a couple of times and wiped his eyes.

"So when you said that I was delivering something to you that you dearly desired, you meant my life, right?"

"No," he said, wiping his nose on his sleeve. That was blasphemous! His suit was gorgeous. I groaned at the vision of it but held my tongue. "I was referring to the dragon named Claire."

"What about her?"

"She's the one for me," he said, staring off into the distance with a look of love on his face. "She has never come down to this level because she knows that I will ensnare her for all eternity."

Interesting.

"You will?"

"Dragons cannot escape my eyes," he explained, "and with one such as Claire, I shall use them to captivate her."

That was cool, if he could manage it. I didn't know much about basilisks, other than that entire "don't look in their eyes" shit they drilled into us at the academy, but I assumed he had some way of taming a dragon.

"I do," he said, proving that he could read my thoughts as well as the valkyries. "We met at a conference in the Netherworld. She was horrible, vile, deceitful...I fell in love instantly. But she had no desire to be with me." His smile returned and he glanced back the way we came. "But I sense her in my lair now. She has arrived and she will stay here for all eternity, loving me as I have loved her."

I kind of felt bad for the guy, seeing as how I had kind of gotten to know this Claire chick a bit. She wasn't bound to love anyone but herself. She'd use Basil and then spit him out.

"You know that she's—"

"I know her very well, Ian," Basil said. "Better than she knows herself, in fact. But it doesn't matter, for in my lair, she will succumb to me and will worship me. It is why I was placed in the deepest level of them all, and why I am not allowed to use my powers anywhere other than here."

"What do you mean?" I said as I saw Claire coming down the massive escalator.

"My eyes have magic over dragons," he explained as he stared dreamily up at her. "They cannot resist me."

"Seriously?"

"Absolutely."

I looked at the exit and then I looked back at Claire.

"Okay," I said, "this I gotta see."

CHAPTER 33

*C*laire came up the rocks, hopping from one to the other with grace and agility.

She didn't slip or teeter even once.

Bitch.

"Come hither, my lovely Claire," said Basil with his arms out wide. "We shall finally be together."

"Yeah," she said without looking up, "I don't think so, yellow eyes."

"Huh?"

Claire reached into her pocket and pulled out a pair of sunglasses that looked identical to the ones Basil had been wearing when I'd first met him.

She slipped them on.

"Shit," said Basil. "Where did you get those?"

"Your mom."

I tried not to, but I laughed.

"Damn her," Basil cursed, stomping his foot. "She's never been supportive of my work."

My laughter died off. "Wait, really? Your mom makes these?"

"She knows I can't use my glare on people if they're wearing those damn things," Basil replied with a sneer, "so she sells them for ten thousand gold each."

"Wow."

That put me in a very bad situation.

While I wasn't worried about Basil, I knew damn well that Claire could best me in a fight. It'd be tough, but she'd likely win in the end. And with this level being quite cavernous, she could even go into full dragon mode if she wanted to. She wouldn't, though, because I'd be able to get to the exit before her transformation completed.

"You may as well just give up," Claire said with a smirk. "I have no problem fighting you, but we both know I'll win."

I took out Boomy and pointed it at her chest.

She laughed.

"You know it's not going to get through my armor."

I moved it to point at her head.

"Oh," she said.

Just as I was about to fire, Basil yelled "No!" and pushed my arm up as I pulled the trigger. The bullet ricocheted off the ceiling and headed off through the level as Boomy dislodged from my hand and clanked on the ground, coming precariously close to falling into the lava.

Claire was already on the move, diving for my mid-section.

Just as she tackled me, I threw a right jab at Basil, knocking him on his ass.

You don't touch my fucking gun.

I rolled with the tackle and launched Claire off me in the process.

Had she been any other fighter, she would have landed on her back; instead, she twisted in midair and hit the ground feet-first.

Impressive.

Basil had gotten back to his feet and was rubbing his cheek. I gave him a "don't screw with me" look and he backed away. Good thing, too, because I had no qualms about dumping his disturbing ass into the lava. Again, I didn't know if that would have done anything to him, but seeing that he was getting as far away from me as possible, I had a feeling him falling into that pit wouldn't be good for his flawless complexion.

Claire was on the move again. She stepped forward and threw a roundhouse kick toward my head. I backed off just enough and then went to take out her other leg. She hopped during rotation and cleared my sweep attempt.

As if in a deathly dance, we parried back and forth, kicking and punching like two kung-fu warriors on one of those movies from the eighties.

I was tempted to say, "My temple is the best," but I refrained.

This was no time for jokes.

She jumped in close, giving me the chance to dislodge the shades she was wearing.

I caught a hard punch to the gut, knocking the wind out of me, but if I could get those glasses off, it'd be worth it.

They didn't budge when I grabbed at them.

Claire chuckled as I doubled over and hit the ground.

"They're magical, asshole," she said as I fought to catch my breath.

She kicked me on the side of my head, laying me flat out and leaving me there groaning.

Then she stepped over me.

"Besides me, only a wizard or a mage can take these shades off my head."

That's when a familiar voice announced, "Perfect."

Claire's head jolted up just as a bright spell split her sunglasses in two. An ice ball followed that, knocking Claire back as I kicked out at her legs.

She fell down and slid away as the momentum of frozen spells crashed against her.

Finally, she came to a stop right next to Basil.

His grin was huge as he lovingly looked down into Claire's eyes.

"Fuck," she said an instant before her armor faded away.

She convulsed slightly, clearly fighting against those yellow swirling eyes.

Finally, she went still.

Then her demeanor changed radically.

"My love," she said, reaching out and stroking his hair.

Basil did a fist-pump and whispered, "Yes."

I got to my feet and glanced over at my crew.

"Thank you," I said after verifying they were all okay. Then I waved at them. "Don't look in his eyes. He's a basilisk."

They immediately glanced away.

"Are you okay?" Rachel asked. "I was…I mean, *we* were worried."

"It's been…interesting," I answered. "I hope you guys didn't have to go through what I just went through."

"We just had to navigate through a bunch of cliffs and such," Chuck stated. "Wasn't that bad. Just took a while."

"Good."

Now wasn't the time to get into my little adventure. Frankly, it was probably never going to be the time. I raised an eyebrow at myself. At least I finally had something I could talk about with Dr. Vernon, assuming we weren't too busy boning. I scratched my head at that thought, wondering how she'd feel about hanging out with valkyries.

Rachel tilted her head at me, rolled her eyes, and scoffed. "What?"

"You got laid," she said. "You're in the nine levels and you got laid."

I held up my hands in surrender. "It's not what you think." Then I flinched, frowned, and lowered my hands. "And so what if I did?"

"Ugh," was her only reply.

"Anyway," I said, spinning back toward Basil, "you got what you wanted, right?"

He was nodding happily as Claire massaged his shoulders.

"Then how about helping us get topside without having to go through too much trouble? Is that possible?"

"Oh, sure," Basil said. He looked to be incredibly happy at the moment. "I have an elevator over here that will take you straight to the top."

"You're kidding," I replied as we followed him over to an opening in the wall. Sure enough, there were metal doors with an "up" button seated on a panel to the right of them. "You're not kidding."

"Nope."

He then donned his sunglasses and looked up at me. Obviously this was unnecessary since I was clearly immune to his gaze, but the rest of my crew wasn't, so I appreciated the sentiment.

I picked up Boomy and tucked him safely home.

"You have done me a great service, Ian," he stated. "While I don't appreciate that you punched me in the face, I understand why you did it and therefore forgive you."

"Gee, thanks."

"You're welcome."

The elevator doors opened and everyone piled in.

"Good luck to you all," Basil said.

"Thanks, pal," I replied, glancing over at Claire, recognizing she'd never be a thorn in my side again. While I wasn't a fan of this trickery that the basilisk had used on her, I found solace in the fact that it couldn't have happened to a nicer dragon. "Have a great honeymoon."

CHAPTER 34

*I*t was great to be back on top.

    With nobody around to read my mind, it was okay to think things like that again.

The air was still sulfury, but at least I was no longer trapped in the nine levels. That would take years of "therapy" to unravel, if I was lucky.

"Nobody was hurt or anything, right?" I asked as I gave my crew the onceover.

They all shook their heads.

"Good." I looked off toward the tower that housed our resident wizard and his fake girlfriend. "We have to get over there and stop that warped dragon chick from doing whatever it is she's planning on doing to Warren."

"That's a long walk," said Rachel, standing a good distance from me.

That was odd.

"And it's not like there are any taxis around here," noted Felicia.

"No," agreed Turbo as he fluttered in front of everyone, "but there is a transit system, of sorts. It was installed during the age before the Badlands seceded from Netherworld Proper."

"Where is it?"

"I'm not certain," he said. "I'd have to get my bearings first."

With that, he whipped out a small device and started tapping it, hitting it, and cursing at it. I wasn't one who was known for being top of the class when it came to technology, but I got the feeling that the only action that was of any use was the tapping.

Turbo flew off in a couple of directions while yelling at the—as he called it—"infernal device!"

Finally, he came back and landed on Harvey's shoulder. Harvey was still partially in werebear mode. Since he wasn't fully bear, he looked kind of like what you might expect Bigfoot to look like.

"Okay, it's that way."

"Toward the tower?" I said.

"That's where I'm pointin', Chief."

I sighed. "Right. How far?"

"About five miles."

We all turned to start walking and then stopped.

"Sorry, did you say five miles?"

"Yep."

"So you are telling us," began Griff, "that we are to walk five miles in that direction, which clearly overshoots the tower by at least two miles, in order to acquire transportation so that we may come *back* to the tower after passing it on foot?"

Turbo adjusted his little tie. "Well, when you put it *that* way..." He trailed off.

"All right, fine," I said after staring at Turbo for a couple of seconds, "get your guns ready. Mages, keep your magic to a minimum. We may need it. Harvey, if you could keep the partial bear thing going, that'd be a good idea, too. We need your strength, but we also need you to have your wits about you."

He nodded and grunted in response.

Close enough.

I took point and started heading toward the tower. Distances were tricky on planes like this because everything was almost uniform. It was like looking at a mountain and thinking it's only a mile or so away but it turns out that it's more like twenty miles away.

Hopefully Turbo's device was correct.

"Harvey," I called back, signaling him forward, "how good is your nose for stuff like this?"

Grunt.

"Okay, I don't speak werebear, so one grunt for yes, two for no. Got it?"

Grunt.

"Good. Is your nose good for smelling and tracking and all that?"

Grunt.

"As good as a werewolf?"

Grunt grunt.

I glanced back at Felicia, thinking it may be best if she changed over to her werewolf form. But I needed her to keep her Desert Eagle at the ready. She couldn't do both, and I wasn't sure how good Harvey was at using weapons.

Hopefully Harvey's sense of smell would be good enough.

"It'll have to do," I said. "Keep your nose in the air and let us know if you catch scent of anything that isn't us."

Grunt.

"I think he understood me," I said to the team through the connector.

"I did," answered Harvey back through the connector.

I stopped and bit my lip.

He turned around. "What?"

"If you could speak without grunts through the connector, why didn't you just do that in the first place?"

"Oh, yeah," he replied with a sheepish grin, which looked pretty funny in his partial-bear situation. "Sorry."

I motioned for him to continue leading the way.

We moved slowly and consistently across the terrain, keeping our eyes, noses, and whatever other senses we could use actively set to scan for trouble.

"Hello there," a grizzly voice said from the top of a small cliff to our right.

Everyone spun and trained their weapons on the creature standing above us.

He or she or whatever it was put its hands up.

I hadn't seen one of these things in a long, long time, and even then it was only in pictures. In fact, those pictures were shown to us by way of paintings or drawings because nobody had any actual photographs of the things. Or if they did, they were kept pretty tightly under wraps. In a nutshell, this creature was to the supernatural community as aliens were to normals. Some people believed they existed, but there was no generally available physical evidence to prove it, meaning that everyone who claimed to see one was either nuts, discredited, or both.

The beast was roughly the size of Harvey, meaning it was pretty tall and quite burly. Its eyes were black and its skin was brownish green, where you could see skin. Most of it was covered under a tan robe that was kept in place with a large, wide leather belt. It carried a gnarled staff that had a skull on its end.

But the things that really stood out were the tusks sticking up from its lower jaw.

"That's a fucking orc," Jasmine whispered. "Right?"

Grunt.

CHAPTER 35

The orc jumped from the cliff face and landed with a loud thump, barely bending its knees upon impact.

Impressive.

From our new perspective, it was clear that he was much larger than Harvey. About a half-head taller and nearly twice as wide. The damn thing's arms looked like my thighs.

"My name is Trezgel," he said while holding out his hand to Harvey. "You must be the leader of this team?"

Grunt grunt.

Trezgel pursed his lips as best as a tusk-jawed orc could. "I'm sorry, I don't speak grunt."

"I'm the leader," I said, stepping up. "My name is Ian Dex."

"*You* are the leader?" His eyes ran over me. "That's impressive."

"Why?"

The orc motioned toward Harvey. "Because this one looks to be capable of besting you in most any challenge."

I was going to argue the point, but from an orc's perspective, physical prowess was the primary indicator of power…at least according to what little information there was on the beasts. It was said they fought to the death to determine who would rule and that any orc may challenge that leadership at any time. Of course, the records also noted that before the Badlands seceded from Netherworld Proper, the orcs had been completely eradicated.

Apparently not.

"Looks can be deceiving," I said without malice. "Now, how may we assist you?"

"I believe it is I who can assist you, Ian Dex."

"Just call me Ian," I said, growing tired of everyone down here using my full name. "And how can you help us, again?"

Trezgel nodded with a slight bow and turned slightly to the side while bringing his arm up in a wide arc.

"You seek the tower," he stated.

"How'd you know that?" asked Rachel.

The orc jolted and gave me a strong stare. He looked as though he'd just eaten one too many tacos.

"You allow your females to speak?"

"He *allows* us to speak?" Rachel snarled.

"Careful, orc," Jasmine stated darkly.

"I'll put my foot in your ass," agreed Felicia.

By now the orc appeared as though he'd been kicked right in the marbles. It was clear that orcs hadn't caught up to humanity in the realm of equality.

"It seems as though our cultures are vastly different, Trezgel," I said, trying to hold back my mirth. "Let's just say that we *try* to consider ourselves equal in every way. We don't always succeed, and there are those of us who are less evolved than others, but we do try."

His brow creased. "Was that an inference that orcs are not as evolved as your kind?"

"Not at all," I replied with haste, although it frankly *was* an inference that humans were more evolved. "I was merely comparing members of our own kind to each other."

"You're *certain* that's what you meant?"

"I'm certain."

He stepped up and began peering into my eyes, leaning his head this way and that as if seeking to discover whether I was telling the truth or not. I continued staring back into his eyes, not glancing away even for a moment.

"Okay," he said with a slow nod. "Okay."

It didn't seem as though he really believed me, and he was right not to. Fact was that I wasn't a fan of people who worked to diminish the role of others due to gender, race, sexual orientation, and so on.

"Anyway," I said, looking past him and up at the tower in the distance, "you were saying that you could help us?"

"Indeed," he replied, softening a bit. "I can guide you to the tower."

"Why would you do that?" said Rachel.

Trezgel flinched again and looked at me, but then after clearly wrestling with some internal conflict, he said, "Because you will not survive the trip without my protection."

"And why would we need your protection?" said Chuck.

Grunt, agreed Harvey.

"This land is overrun by various creatures who will do what they can to destroy you." He stood tall. "They fear me, though, and will therefore allow you safe passage."

"But why?" I asked.

His eyes darted about. "I just told you why. They fear me and therefore—"

"Sorry," I interrupted, "I mean *why* would you help us? What's in it for you?"

"Ah, I see," he said with a firm nod. "As to that, I would ask for two things."

Here it comes. "Go on."

"Your wrist ornament," he said, pointing at my Calibre de Cartier, a watch that wouldn't possibly fit him, "and that one's hat," he finished while pointing at Chuck.

"Chief?" Chuck said through the connector without saying anything aloud. "I can't give up my hat."

"Would you rather give up your life?" I countered.

"Damn it."

Something told me that this orc wanted more from us than my watch and Chuck's hat, but that just meant we'd have to stay on our toes. And maybe, just maybe, Trezgel could get us safely to the tower. If he did, he could have exactly what he'd asked for. Hats and watches were easily replaced; members of my team were not.

"Fine," I said finally. "We have a deal."

Trezgel's eyes lit up.

"Excellent," he said as he spun on his heel. "Follow me."

CHAPTER 36

The trip to the tower was brisk because Trezgel's stride was crazy long, even though it seemed like he was going out of his way to walk slowly.

"Obviously we can't trust this guy," I said through the connector. "I'm assuming all of you have your weapons and magic ready?"

There was a general consensus.

I then targeted the connector to Rachel.

"You okay?" I asked. "You've been acting a bit odd since we met back up by the basilisk."

"I'm fine," she replied, not sounding fine at all.

"You sure?"

"I'm fine."

That solidified it. She wasn't fine, but I wasn't going to push it either.

"Okay," I said. "Just making sure." I then connected to Felicia and Jasmine. "Something up with Rachel that you guys know about?"

"What do you mean?" asked Jasmine.

"Well," I replied, noting the distance that Rachel was

walking away from me, "look at her. She's usually right next to me."

"Huh," Felicia said. "You're right. I hadn't noticed that. Why don't you just ask her?"

"I did. She said nothing was wrong, but it's obvious that something is wrong."

"Yep," agreed Jasmine. "You want me to—?"

"No," I interrupted. "She'll know it was me who asked you to ask her. I'll just let it go. If she doesn't want to tell me what's up, I'll respect that as long as it doesn't interfere with our work."

I opened up to the group on the connector again, but I didn't say anything.

It was obvious that I'd done something wrong. Seemed I always did. But I had no idea what precisely that was. If I was to guess, though, I'd have to say it was because she knew I'd gotten laid along the way in the nine levels. That was when she seemed to get all irked at me.

Ah, well, nothing I could do about it.

Besides, we were in the middle of the Badlands and I had to focus on things a little more pressing than why Rachel was pissed off at me at the moment. There'd be plenty of time to delve into that if we made it out of here alive. It wasn't like this was the first time she'd been irritated at me and—unless we met our final doom here—it wouldn't be the last.

I picked up my pace until I was walking alongside Harvey and Trezgel.

Harvey was padding beside the orc as if he were the thing's pet. It was kind of odd, but Trezgel either didn't mind or didn't care. I had the feeling it was a bit of both.

"Forgive my ignorance," I said as tactfully as I could, "but I was under the impression that orcs were snuffed out via genocide."

"Almost," he said, clearly not offended. "As you can see,

the mission to obliterate my race was not completely successful."

"Indeed."

He continued on in silence. It seemed that nobody was interested in providing much detail with me at the moment.

That was fine. I'd just scan the horizon and gain my bearings.

The Badlands were surprisingly comfortable as far as temperature went. I would have expected it to be searingly hot—it was very red, after all. But the climate was nice. Warm, yes, but not unpleasantly so.

It was like the desert without the blazing sun and without all the sand. The ground was firm, mostly. There were cracks here and there and the occasional mud pit could be seen bubbling, but there wasn't all the fire and brimstone like they taught in Netherworld Proper. There were even kids' shows that warned of the burning heat, slithering monsters, and firestorms. Not like the firestorms they talked about in California, either. These were the type of storms where literal fire came down from the sky.

That made me look up.

Being in the Netherworld, Badlands or not, you wouldn't think there'd be a sky. But there was. That's because this wasn't a place located *inside* of Earth. It was a dimensional shift. A thin coat of reality that separated the two worlds. If that reality ever merged, both sides would be in for one hell of a ride. Fortunately, according to the best scientific minds, the merging of the two realities was impossible.

"Halt," said Trezgel as he came to a stop, holding out his staff.

We complied.

The tower wasn't far now, and it was massive. It was the kind of tower you read about in books where wizards ruled worlds and dragons hoarded fine jewels. It was the kind of tower you *knew* contained rituals where people were sacrificed so that the powerful could gain more power. The place was evil. I could feel it. Hell, I could *see* it. The walls were obsidian with streaks of red that led all the way up to its point. Evil, I tell ya.

"Before we proceed," said Trezgel in a way that made me think he was having second thoughts about helping us go any farther, "explain to me why you wish to enter the tower."

I glanced at the others but decided to go ahead and let Trezgel know why we needed to get there. I couldn't see any reason why he shouldn't know.

"My lead wizard has been taken by the dragon known as Charlotte," I answered. "I don't know what her purpose is, but I can't imagine it's good."

"No," he agreed, "it won't be. Charlotte is evil incarnate. Just look at her tower."

"Yeah, she does seem like a real bitch."

"You don't know the half of it."

He sighed and seemed to sag. Then he looked up at the black building, back at us, and then down at the ground. Finally, he began rubbing the back of his neck with his free hand.

"I have an admission to make," he said in a drawn voice.

"Okay?"

"I have no use for your wrist adornment or that man's hat," he said slowly. "I have brought you here because the dragon queen instructed me to do so in the event that you somehow bested her children."

I had Boomy out in a flash.

CHAPTER 37

*T*rezgel didn't even put up his hands. He merely gazed down at the weapon and then pointed to his right.

We all looked over the lip of the hill that connected to the tower.

"Shit," I said.

"Damn," agreed Jasmine.

"Fuck," Felicia hissed.

"Golly," stated Griff.

Grunt.

There were easily five thousand orcs in the valley below. They were all standing like frozen soldiers waiting for battle.

"There's some type of magical sheen over them," Rachel said through the connector, glancing at everyone but me. "My guess is that they're in some kind of stasis."

"It's actually a refraining shield," Griff corrected. "These require a wizard's touch due to the amount of preparation and building of power. My assumption is the fellow who brought Warren to this tower masterminded it."

I took a quick look at Trezgel. "Can the orc open it?"

"Not likely," Griff replied, "unless he has been given a key."

"A key?"

"Correct. When wizards create something like this, it's usually done at the command of someone who is pulling their strings."

"Charlotte," said Jasmine.

"That would be my assumption," Griff acknowledged. "Since she would not possess the level of magic necessary to unravel such a spell, the wizard would make her a key."

I scanned Trezgel to see if he had a key on his person. There was nothing obvious, but that didn't mean it wasn't hidden in a pocket or something. Plus, I assumed it didn't have to be key-shaped. It could probably be anything.

"He wouldn't have it," Griff stated again. "The dragon is far too cunning to allow an underling to carry such power."

"Are you sure?" Rachel asked.

"I obviously cannot be one hundred percent certain," Griff admitted, "but the odds of him carrying the item are rather low."

We were Vegas cops. Odds were everything when it came to our jurisdiction.

I agreed with Griff on this, too.

Charlotte wasn't going to let some peon walk around with the ability to unleash this many warriors. First off, she was a dragon, which meant she had an ego the size of the Badlands. Giving power to anyone else would be almost painful for her. Giving a key to Trezgel would be considered delegation. Dragons didn't delegate, they commanded. Secondly, dragons were paranoid. Charlotte would immediately worry that the orc was going to try and turn this army against her, so there's no way she'd provide him a key that could allow for such potentiality.

"You see," continued Griff, "all of those orcs are nothing but lifeless shells. They are merely physical at this point."

"You mean they're dead?" said Chuck.

"They've never been alive," answered Griff. "The moment that the key-wielder opens the gate, life will fill them and they will attach to the one who freed them."

That solidified point number two in my thinking. If Trezgel opened that gate, *he* would own those orcs.

"That's pretty sick," Felicia noted.

We all continued staring at the stagnate creatures for another couple of seconds.

"That is an impressive sight," I said aloud, bringing up my eyes to meet Trezgel's.

"Yes."

"Unfortunately, they're in stasis of some kind and you have no way of releasing them."

He nodded without hesitation. "That is correct."

That caught me off guard. I was fully expecting him to bluff at this point.

"Huh?"

"The dragon queen would never provide a key to an underling," he declared. "It's not in their nature to be so trusting."

"Then what's going on?" said Chuck. "You brought us this far and said you don't want my hat, but then you show us this. Obviously you've got something up your sleeve."

We all nodded at Chuck's comment.

Trezgel breathed heavily. "My point in showing you this is to explain what I'm going to do next."

I aimed Boomy carefully and prepared to pull the trigger.

"What?" I said in a challenging tone.

"I'm going to show you the *actual* path into the tower," he said, turning and walking away. "Originally, I was instructed to bring you through the main entrance." We all followed him, keeping our weapons at the ready. "Once inside, I would have slipped through a secret room and locked it. The main doors would seal up and you'd all be trapped. Then the floor would drop and everyone would fall into the tomb of flames, which is located under the castle. There is no escape."

"Sounds lovely," I said, wincing at the thought. "So why aren't you doing that, again?" I then paused. "I mean, *thanks*, but…why?"

He stopped and pointed again in the direction of the orcs.

"Those are my people, Ian," he said, sounding almost sad. "The dragon queen doesn't care if they live or die. I do. With your help, we may be able to save your wizard and my people at the same time."

"Ah."

Trezgel began his walk again.

He was taking us to the side of the tower, castle, or whatever the hell it was called. Frankly, it looked kind of like both. Castle on the bottom and a massive tower on the top.

We approached one of the walls and Trezgel began putting his hands on various rocks, using different fingers and different positions with each one. It was obviously some type of passcode that, when entered correctly, opened a secret entrance. I shuddered to think what would happen if you got the wrong code, and I didn't see any "forgot your password?" notices anywhere.

"Be on your toes," I said through the connector, even though it didn't need saying. My crew was made up of professionals who had seen more action than I had. But it's the kind of thing chiefs said. "I have no clue what this dude is planning, but if he double-crosses us, let's at least kill his ass before we die."

"Agreed," said Turbo. "I already have my gun trained on him, Chief."

A quick peek showed that Turbo's weapon was out and

focused. Again, I had no doubt that the little gun was dangerous as hell, especially considering that Turbo had built the damn thing, but it was difficult to rationalize.

It's like trying to wrap your head around the fact that if you took a cubic meter of a neutron star, it would weigh roughly the same as the entirety of the Atlantic Ocean. I saw that on a PBS show while eating ice cream and wallowing in despair after becoming chief and realizing that I could no longer bone the chicks on my crew.

A piece of the wall glowed for a moment and then disappeared.

"If you will please follow me," said Trezgel, "I will lead you safely to the queen."

CHAPTER 38

*W*e followed the orc into the castle, fully expecting to be attacked the instant we were all inside.

That didn't happen.

He walked up through a winding staircase that made me think that I'd not been spending enough time at the gym as of late. I was never one who was fond of running on a treadmill or doing the stair stepper machine, but this made those options almost appealing. Trezgel's tree-trunk legs could probably go up and down these steps all day, but mine were burning. I couldn't even imagine how Griff was handling this, seeing as how he was the oldest member of my crew.

"You okay, Griff?"

"Couldn't be better," he replied in an almost chipper voice. "I was just explaining to Chuck how glad I was that I've been employing the use of the stair climber machine at our condominium complex."

"Right."

After what seemed an eternity, we finally reached the top of our ascent and the orc opened a door.

We stepped through and our breath caught.

If it was Trezgel's goal to tire us out to the point where we couldn't even hope to put up a struggle, he had succeeded. Harvey, Turbo, and Griff all appeared none the worse for wear, but the rest of us were hating life.

"You should really consider putting an elevator in this place," I suggested through gasps.

"The dragon queen would not allow such things," the orc replied. "She flies, as you may recall, and dragons are not exactly known for doling out sympathy to anyone."

I nodded, still bending at the waist with my hands on my thighs. "What about that old wizard of hers, though?"

"He has developed his own magical lift, and he does not share it, either." Trezgel glanced out one of the windows. "If you wish to save your wizard friend, we must hurry. Time is growing short for him, I'm afraid."

"How do you know that?" asked Rachel.

"The glow emanating from the dragon queen's lair is growing."

I pushed myself to full height and released a loud "Phew!" The rest of my team did essentially the same thing, but in their own way.

"Lead on," I said tiredly, knowing that my legs would recover in a matter of minutes. "And no funny stuff."

Trezgel did not reply.

We exited the small room we were in and padded down a hallway that was adorned with jewels and runes.

"What are these runes?" Jasmine asked Trezgel.

"They are used to notify the dragon queen of approaching people."

"So they're notification runes," Felicia said with a laugh.

She then stared up at Trezgel, who had stopped at another door. "Kind of hard to sneak up on Charlotte if she knows we're coming, asshole."

"They are in the midst of a ritual," he replied, clearly not offended by the name-calling. "The runes will be nothing but background noise to them." He swallowed and sighed heavily. "I've seen this ritual firsthand when the dragon queen and the wizard created my people."

"Wait, wait, wait," I replied as his words hit me. "You're telling us that the massive army of orcs out there was created by Charlotte *and* Gandalf?"

Trezgel frowned. "I'm sorry, but who is Gandalf?"

"He means Melvin," Rachel corrected while rolling her eyes.

"I see," Trezgel said. "Yes, they were both responsible for the creation."

"But you said you *saw* this happen, right?" said Turbo. "If you were created with them, how could you—"

"I was not created with them," interrupted Trezgel. "I was the seed that allowed their creation. I have lived the life of a nomad since Netherworld Proper attempted to eradicate my race. I've been hiding in caves and living off of what little I had." His words were heavy. "The dragon queen found me and promised to rebuild my people if I would allow her to do so." His face tightened. "But she deceived me. All she wanted was an army so that she could bring them into the Overworld and build a kingdom."

"What the what?" I said, blinking. "She's creating a portal to bring the orcs through?"

"Yes, Ian," Trezgel said with a slow nod. "That's why she needed your wizard. His essence was required to power the rift."

I grimaced. "What do you mean by his 'essence'?"

"He's talking about his personal energy, you freak," Rachel said more venomously than I was used to. "Honestly, do you have to have your mind in the gutter all the time?"

I blanched.

"Not *all* the time, no," I retaliated. "But Charlotte *was* coming on to Warren in the Overworld, right? And while *you* may be a mage and have a deep understanding of all this shit, I don't."

She thinned her eyes for a moment and then looked away.

I had no idea what the fuck her problem was, but it was getting old.

I opened a direct connection to her. "Look, if you want to be a bitch to me about whatever the hell you're pissed off about, fine, but do it on your own time. Right now we're working, so get over it."

"Fuck you."

Not unexpected.

"When this portal opens," asked Griff as the space between Rachel and I grew thicker with each passing moment, "what will happen?"

"The dragon queen will fly down and release my people. They will follow her to a portal that will connect with some place she has been calling 'the Strip,' and they will bring it to its knees."

Chuck adjusted his hat. "You know where in this castle that portal is going to open?"

"Not specifically," Trezgel answered. "She won't say."

"Just doesn't want anyone else to get through the portal before she does," said Griff as he tapped his chin. "This is her moment of glory. Dragons are not known for sharing those."

Trezgel gave a single nod to acknowledge that what Griff had said was accurate. Not that I had any doubt, seeing that Griff was the most experienced mage in the Vegas PPD, but it was always good to have a confirmation.

"Then I guess we'd better stop her," I stated, motioning Trezgel to open the door.

CHAPTER 39

The room was awash with lights of all different shades and hues. It was like standing in a Faraday cage.

Yes, I watched *a lot* of PBS shows whenever I get depressed. Don't judge me.

Warren was on a table, strapped down with his face toward the ceiling. His eyes were closed, but there was an eerie glow around the lids that told me the electricity was flowing through him.

He looked kind of like a scrawny Frankenstein who went on a pot-brownie and 'shroom kick while cranking up Pink Floyd.

Melvin, the old wizard, had his staff raised with one hand while his empty hand was swiftly drawing designs in the air. They were obviously magical symbols of some kind. Each one that he drew flashed momentarily and then flew into Warren like a projectile. In turn, my chief wizard jolted slightly after every hit.

Charlotte was back in her human form, facing away from us and acting like the third point of a magical triangle. The mini bolts of lightning bounced from Warren to her when Melvin launched a symbol into the fray.

Another fragment of the energy then got sucked up into a shiny metal ball that sat above them all.

I pulled up Boomy and fired it right at Charlotte's back.

She lurched forward with the hit, but the breaker bullet bounced off, signaling that she either had her armor up or that the ritual was protecting her. But Charlotte didn't spin around or anything. She just stepped back into position and continued on with whatever it was they were doing.

My guess was that she was in a trance of some kind.

"Take out Melvin," I yelled over the crackling noise that filled the room.

Felicia and Chuck fired, but their bullets bounced away without even disturbing the old wizard.

"I'll do it," cried Turbo as he pulled the trigger on his miniature gun.

A *boom* reverberated. The kick of the weapon blew the pixie back with such force that he smacked into the wall behind him and slid down it.

The bullet didn't fully penetrate the shield, but it was enough to distract Melvin. This, in turn, brought Charlotte out of her trance.

She spun and looked at us.

"You dare to betray me?" the dragon queen screamed at Trezgel. "You are nothing but a worm!"

"Technically," I said, raising a finger, "you're a wurm, right? You know, with a 'u.'"

Everyone stopped what they were doing and looked at me.

"I watch PBS whenever..." I began and then stopped myself. "Never mind." I glowered and said, "Stop what you're doing or die."

"Phnop phnut phnyou're phnoing phnor phnie,"

Charlotte spat back in a childish mocking way, much like Rachel did to me from time to time. "I'm not afraid of you insignificant pieces of shit."

"Your kids are dead," I said, hoping to elicit some response from her. "Maybe if *they'd* had a little fear, they'd still—"

"Yawn," she replied, unfazed. "They were worthless anyway, except for Claire, that is." A stream of electricity struck her on the shoulder. Her face showed a look of pleasure at this. "How did they die?"

"Uh..." I squinted at her, thinking that if she didn't care about them dying, why would she want to know *how* they'd each met their doom? "Well, Stan had his head bitten off by the demon queen."

"He pissed off Lucy Für, eh?" she said, smirking.

I opened the connector and said, "Look for ways to get to them while I keep her occupied."

"And what about Wilbur?"

"Died in a sex contest."

Rachel gave me a sharp look and shook her head.

So that *was* the problem! I knew it. Why it bugged her down here and not in the Overworld, I couldn't say, but clearly she was pissed. Then again, she always gave me shit about my sexual escapades, so what made this one so different in her eyes?

"A what?"

"The valkyries," I explained as chatter along the connector made it clear that my crew had found a potential hole in the shield. "Uh, I told them that I was no match for a dragon in a fight and since they required fairness, a sexual competition was decided upon."

"So," Charlotte said, blinking at me, "are you saying that you fucked my son to death?"

"*I* didn't," I replied as my entire team turned to look at

me. "The satyrs did. Well, they didn't technically either, but me and Claire were just better boning each other than the satyrs and Wilbur were at boning each other." Even with all the electricity bouncing around the room, it felt like the place went silent at that moment. "He died happy, if that matters."

"Why would it?" she asked.

"Because you're his mother and..." I looked at her and saw the confused expression on her face. "Right. Anyway, Claire didn't die, but she ended up marrying Basil, so she's kind of eternally trapped."

"I warned her to buy sunglasses from Basil's mother," Charlotte said. "But did she listen? No." She shook her head. "Kids these days."

"Actually," I corrected her, "she *did* buy the glasses, but my team magically removed them, which gave Basil the ability to use his eyes on her."

Charlotte crossed her arms and pursed her lips. Her eyebrows were up and she appeared rather impressed.

"Interesting," she said, her eyes darting to each member of my team. Obviously she wasn't going to be able to take us as lightly as she assumed she could. If we took out all three of her kids, certainly we were at least *some* level of threat that should be respected.

Felicia stopped her study of the room and looked back at me. "So, you boned the dragon and then she married the basilisk?"

"Yeah, why?"

"Nothing," she chuckled. "Just that you were essentially her bachelorette party."

"Oh, yeah," I said as a sinister grin crept onto my face. "Cool."

Rachel scowled. "Perv."

My grin faded away.

"Anyway," I said, redirecting my attention back to Charlotte, "the fact is that I was responsible for killing two of your kids, and my team and I got your third child eternally trapped in the ninth level." I raised Boomy and aimed it at her forehead. "Do you really think you can beat us?"

It was her turn to grin sinisterly.

CHAPTER 40

*O*kay, so maybe it wasn't the best idea to challenge a dragon like that, but sometimes you gotta take one for the team.

This is what went through my mind as I slid down the same wall that Turbo had slid down after firing off his gun. He was sitting next to me rubbing his head while I rubbed the indent on my chest that was caused by the boot of one Charlotte the Dragon.

She was fast. Like *Haste* fast.

"Ouch," I said as Charlotte zipped around the room, punching and kicking my team as if they were standing still.

I had to do something, but I didn't know what.

Sheesh, that crazy dragon bitch was even giving Trezgel a solid ass-kicking, and he looked to be built out of granite.

Time.

The thought rang out from my subconscious mind, much like *Flashes* had done when we'd been hunting Shitfaced Fred a while back.

A vision of Dr. Vernon during her extended orgasm came to mind. That had been something to see, certainly, but how did the *Time* thing play into stopping Charlotte? I suppose I *could* use *Time* to stop everything and give her a lengthy orgasm.

Ummm...no.

She didn't deserve it.

Time.

Yeah, yeah, yeah. It wasn't like I didn't hear myself the first time around. But what was I supposed to do with it?

I studied the room as bodies flew about. There was no way I could get past that infernal dragon, and even if I did, how was I to get to the table and free Warren with all that electricity flying about?

A thought struck.

"Turbo," I said, plucking the pixie on the head gently.

"Hey," he answered with a frown. "Watch it."

"Sorry. Listen, if I can get you through that..." I pointed at the swirling energy.

"Maelstrom?"

I shrugged. "Sure, okay. If I can get you through it, would you be able to use your gun to blow up the silver ball thing that's sucking up all the energy?"

"Kerpow would make minced meat of that ball," he said while eying his gun lovingly.

"Kerpow?" I said with a chuckle.

"Boomy?" he replied with a chuckle that mocked my own.

"Right."

Now, the real problem was that I didn't know if Turbo was going to be able to manage the time differential alongside of me or if he'd be slowed down with it in much the same way Dr. Vernon had been. During my tryst with my eminent psychologist, I'd lived outside of the time dilation. She hadn't.

"I'm going to slow time," I said to the pixie. "When that

happens, you'll probably be seeing me move super fast. You might want to close your eyes for this."

"Slow time?"

"Exactly," I said as I closed my eyes and calmed my mind.

I recalled the way I'd thought about the word before. The feeling, the inflection, and the desire. Not *that* desire.

Time.

Everything slowed to a crawl.

I picked up Turbo and stuck him in my shirt pocket. There was room. It wasn't like I put pens in there, after all.

While everyone else was moving in slow motion, I was able to go at the same speed as always.

The first thing I did was move Jasmine out of the way from the incoming fist that Charlotte was throwing.

The second thing I did was punch Charlotte in the head, which had to have felt like she'd been hit by a planet.

The third thing I did was stand in front of Rachel and stick my tongue out at her. I probably stood there doing this for far too long, but it felt good to get it out of my system. While her face was moving super slow, I had the sensation that her eyes were in the process of creasing angrily.

No more time to waste.

I had to get Warren off that table and…

And what?

I looked at Melvin.

I looked at Warren.

I looked at Charlotte.

I looked at the energy-sucking metal ball.

"Perfect!"

CHAPTER 41

*M*y first fear was that walking through the electrical field was going to hurt like shit.

It did.

Fortunately, it was just like one of those jolts like you got from touching a rune-protected door. It wasn't fun, and it *could* knock you on your ass if you weren't ready for it, but you'd live. Another fortunate bit was that I'd had the foresight to set Turbo down before attempting to go through. He was still moving at the same speed as the electricity. That meant he'd not be able to step through sections like I could.

I stepped back out and snapped up the little pixie.

The only way he was getting through was if I found a blank area and slid him in. There couldn't be any energy flowing or he'd get thumped. It was like playing a game of Operation, except that this game board could move. Thankfully, time was going so slowly that I got him through safely and then pushed my way back through the field.

Honestly, it wasn't at all pleasant.

I saw a switch next to the old wizard and flicked it off. The energy field died.

To the rest of the room this would look like nothing but a flicker. Their brains wouldn't process the change for at least a half-second in real time, and that was a long way away in my world.

It took me a minute to get the straps off Warren. His face was ashen and his body temperature was cold. I assumed he'd be burning up, but that just made me remember it was *his* energy they were draining.

I got him to the other side of the room and gently set him down.

Then I grabbed Charlotte, who was still slowly falling over from my punch, and shoved her onto the table.

After attaching the straps to her, I took out Boomy and fired at the metal ball. It just ricocheted off of it like I'd expected it would.

Turbo's gun was far too tiny for me to use, though, and that meant I needed to get back to normal time.

"I hope you're ready for this, little dude," I said to him as I picked him up and lined up his shot. "Good thing you kept your eyes shut."

Just like clockwork (pun intended) the effects of *Time* disappeared. It was as though it *knew* when I was done with it.

"Fire!" I yelled.

Turbo raised Kerpow and shot the silver ball. The kick was heavy enough that the little pixie slammed into my chest.

But the shot did the trick.

The ball shattered as Melvin's face contorted and Charlotte screamed.

"What's happening?" yelled the old wizard. Then he pointed at me. "What have you done?"

"Saved my wizard, dick nose," I replied as I launched Turbo toward Harvey.

I then landed a right cross on Melvin's chin, and then flicked the energy switch back on. The rush of power threatened to rip through every fiber of my being as I was caught right in the middle of it.

It hurt like fuck.

"Ian!" Rachel hollered through the connector.

Then she grabbed me and pulled me free of the pain.

We both collapsed, but only Rachel lost consciousness.

Jasmine and Griff rushed over to work on her as I drunkenly pulled myself up and looked back at Melvin and Charlotte.

"Stop the ritual, you stupid son of a bitch," Charlotte was hollering at the old wizard.

"I can't," Melvin spat back while rubbing his jaw from where I'd struck him. "It's too late."

She strained against the restraints, popping them from her arms.

This bitch was *strong*.

Charlotte crossed her arms and began morphing into her full dragon form.

She didn't make it.

A whipping sound like that of a vortex dragged everything that was *inside* the magic field, including the field itself, down to a single point.

Everything.

There was nothing left but the sound of ragged breaths coming from my team and what looked like a marble-sized ball of light floating where the table had once stood.

"What's that?" I asked, pointing with a shaky finger.

As if in answer to my question, the damn thing exploded, blowing all of us back to the sides of the room as a stream of light flew straight down and flooded everything.

Worse, there were chunks of stuff flying all over the place.

Those chunks included bits of Melvin and Charlotte.

I knew this because a talon stuck in my thigh and that immediately caused the word *Flashes* to go through my head as pain raked my body.

"Aw, fuck," I said a nanosecond before everything froze.

CHAPTER 42

I'd been through *Flashes* once before, so I kind of knew what to expect. The first time it'd happened was back when my crew had been dealing with Shitfaced Fred and his zombie apocalypse.

This one didn't feel much different, but obviously Fred wasn't the focus…Charlotte was.

Now, I didn't know how all of this worked, but when it happened with Fred, I'd seen everything from the eyes of an unknown soldier who had been tracking Fred's master, looking to snipe him.

This time, I didn't know whose eyes I was looking through, but he or she seemed to be hazed and following Melvin and Charlotte around inside what appeared to be the tower I was currently seated in.

"The orc is on our side?" asked Melvin in an old man's voice.

"Of course," replied Charlotte. "He knows that the only way his race gains life is if I use the key and free them."

So Griff was right about the orcs just being shells.

Warped.

"He may attempt to wrestle the key away," warned Melvin.

Charlotte scoffed. "He'll die trying."

I recognized the hallway they were walking down. To the right was the room where all the crazy electricity shit had just occurred...well, in my normal time, anyway.

"We must choose the location of the portal."

"I already know where it's going to be, Melvin," Charlotte replied. "I kept it on the lowest level so the orcs will be able to get through it quickly."

"Wise," Melvin replied, nodding. "Time will be of the essence, for certain."

She stopped and eyed the old wizard. "I thought you said that the fabric would be permanently ripped. Is that not true?"

"It is tied to you and that key," Melvin answered, pointing at the silver square that hung from Charlotte's neck. So it *wasn't* key-shaped. "If *you* specifically get through the portal, and if *I* safely get through, and the key as well, the rift will be permanent. If any of those three things don't happen, it will be fleeting."

Smart.

Obviously Melvin knew a thing or two about how dragons worked.

"Are you saying you don't trust me?" Charlotte asked with eyes aflutter.

"Of course I don't," Melvin replied seriously. "Nor should you trust me."

"Never have."

Melvin nodded. "Since we have an understanding, Queen Charlotte, I shall need to know the precise location of where you placed the portal jewel."

In answer, she walked over to a door and opened it. On

the other side was a railing that hung over the edge of a drop all the way down to the bottom of the castle.

"It's on a wire in the center of the expanse," she said, pointing. "If you jump over the railing, you'll fall through the portal. The orcs and I will climb that small set of stairs and leap through."

"Perfect," said Melvin.

Charlotte crossed her arms. "Of course it is."

CHAPTER 43

When *Flashes* ended, I found Harvey had pulled the talon from my leg and everyone was staring down at me with a look of concern in their eyes.

Well, everyone but Warren and Trezgel.

Just like the last time I'd been through a *Flashes* event, I was disoriented and dizzy. But that didn't matter right now. What *did* matter was getting to that portal with the key intact.

"Where is it?" yelled Trezgel as he was throwing things all around the room.

Rachel was the first to ask, "Where is what?"

"The damned key, you stupid female!"

I winced.

"Pardon me?" she said.

Trezgel's eyes were aflame as he spun and approached Rachel. He glared down at her.

She kicked him in the stones.

Now, I specifically used the word "stones" here because apparently that's what orcs had as balls. Either that or they were located in a different place than they were on humans.

Rachel yelled, "Son of a bitch," as she hopped around on one foot while holding her other as if it'd been crushed by a sledgehammer.

Trezgel clearly found Rachel's pain punishment enough because he went back to hunting for the key.

"Guys," I said through the connector, "we have to find the key before he does. If he gets it, he'll be able to release those orcs and give them life."

"Ian is correct," agreed Griff. "We cannot allow that to occur. The problem is that we do not know what the key looks like."

"I do," I stated as I pushed myself up to wobbly feet. "It's square, silver, and is likely attached to a chain since Charlotte was wearing it around her neck."

Everyone stayed put but began inconspicuously looking around the area as Trezgel continued throwing things all over the place. We didn't want him to think we were searching for it, too.

Or did we?

"Trezgel," I yelled, "why do you want this key?"

"To free my people, of course!"

"And what will you do with them?"

His eyes blazed again. "We will take our rightful place as masters of the Netherworld." The orc blinked. "Uh..." His eyes darted around. "I mean, uh, we'll live in harmony and work to be contributing members of society." He scratched innocently on the wall. "I'm sure we'll do a lot of wonderful things, like...uh...gardening and maybe raising livestock."

"Oh, well, that sounds nice," I said, putting on a better acting job than he just had. "Okay, gang, let's help Trezgel find the key so he and his band of orcs can flourish and bring some greenery back to the Badlands." I then winked at the orc. "Maybe they'll even change the name of the place from Badlands to Green Acres when you're done with it, eh?"

"That'd be a dream, of course," he said with the oddest smile I'd ever seen. Then, as if thinking quickly, he turned to Rachel. "I apologize for my behavior before. You must understand that the future of my race is at stake here."

Rachel's face remained tight.

"Play along, please," I said through the connector.

She closed her eyes and released a slow breath. "I totally understand." The words were forced, but Trezgel didn't seem to notice.

"Right," I said, clapping my hands. "Well, let's dig on through and see what we find then, shall we?"

Trezgel resumed his search, but he'd calmed down a fair bit on throwing things around.

"Okay, gang," I said as I looked for the key, "we all know this guy is going to try and do naughty things, so if he gets the key, shoot him, fireball him, and do whatever else you can to destroy his ass. If one of us gets the key, run out of the room, go to the third door on the right, and jump."

"Jump?" Harvey asked, stopping his search and giving me a scared look.

"Yes." Then I hesitated. "Actually, I don't know if the portal even got created."

"What portal?" said Rachel.

I continued picking through things in search of the key as I explained the situation to the others. As soon as I'd finished, Turbo flew from the room and went to check.

"Door is open and there is definitely a portal down there," he said through the connector. "Long drop, though."

Grunt.

"Worry not, Harvey," Griff noted as Warren started coming around, "the fall will be quick, but once we hit the portal it will slow us down and we will land on the other side as if coming to rest on a soft mattress."

Grunt.

"What happened?" asked Warren while rubbing his head. "My eyes are burning like mad."

"Long story," I answered. "We've got a crazed orc in here searching for a key to open the gate that will unleash an army of his kind. Chances are that he'll take them through the portal and try to rule the Overworld. That's my guess, anyway. Oh, and all of this was built by your girlfriend and some wizard named Merlin."

"Melvin," corrected Griff.

"Oh yeah, that's right."

"That didn't seem like a very long story," Warren said. "And am I to assume she's *not* my girlfriend?"

"Well, let's put it this way, she was using you to power the portal," said Jasmine gently. "Sorry."

Warren glanced at her and then went to get up.

"Ouch," he hissed and rubbed his elbow. "What the hell was that?"

Sitting just beneath his arm was the key.

"Don't move," I commanded.

The problem was that everyone on my squad thought that command was meant for them, and so they all froze.

This caught Trezgel's attention.

"Have you found it?" he asked darkly as his eyes bore into mine.

"Uh...well..." I licked my lips and then whipped out Boomy and yelled, "Light his ass up!"

CHAPTER 44

$\mathcal{M}$ayhem ensued as Harvey picked up Warren and began running for the door.

The key dropped to the ground in the process and I swept it up and shoved it into my pocket. If the orc wanted it, he'd have to come and get it.

That didn't make me feel all that swell, actually.

Trezgel was taking our barrage of magic and bullets in stride. It was pressing him back, but there was no way it was stopping him. Clearly, Charlotte and Melvin had done a lot to make certain that the orc would be impenetrable to attacks such as these. And there was an entire army of the damn things.

"Go, go, go!" I yelled, pushing the mages into the hallway as Chuck, Felicia, Turbo, and I kept on firing.

It was Turbo's gun that was doing the best job of keeping the orc at bay. Unfortunately, he could only fire it every few seconds because the kickback kept flinging him at the wall.

Noting that, I tucked in Boomy and picked up Turbo, pointing him in the direction of the orc.

I squeezed.

"Ow," he yelled. "What the fuck?"

"Oh, sorry...shoot him!"

The pixie fired and fired and fired.

I was able to absorb the kick without much fuss and since I was easing Turbo back with each shot, he was able to better manage it as well.

"You two go," I commanded Felicia and Chuck.

They split and I was right behind them, pointing Turbo back at Trezgel for one final shot.

It missed.

The orc was on our asses as I launched over the rail, falling like a bungie jumper without a cord.

"No!" Trezgel yelled as he grabbed my leg after diving after me.

I had spun and was falling with my back to the ground. The orc was right above me, pulling me closer.

We were a split second from the portal when Turbo unleashed a bullet at point-blank range.

rezgel let go as light flashed around me and Turbo, then we smashed into the floor of Charlotte's art gallery.

It felt like what you might imagine jumping from a high dive into an empty pool might feel like.

The portal slammed shut immediately after I'd cleared.

Trezgel also made it through.

Well, his head did anyway.

The rest of him was likely splattered on the castle floor. After all, it was a long drop from the top of that tower.

"So much for it feeling like you're landing on a soft mattress," I said with a groan toward Griff. "That sucked."

"What happened to the orc?" asked Rachel, getting to her feet and looking like she was ready to fight.

I pointed at Trezgel's disembodied head.

She grunted and slumped back to the ground. "Good."

It was all I could do to not yell, "I told you so!" at everyone.

I knew from the start that there was something fishy going on with this Charlotte chick. Yes, I'll admit I was jealous, but there was something more to all of this and I *knew* it.

But what would be the point?

They'd all just say I was being petty. It was *always* my fault, right?

Fuckers.

"So what happens to the orcs in the cage?" asked Harvey, who was returning to his normal self.

"Without that key, they will never be given life," answered Griff.

I dug it out of my pocket and held it up.

"You must hide that away, Ian. It can never be allowed to enter the Badlands."

"I know, Griff," I replied as the key began to glow. "Uh... what's it doing?"

It was getting hot. Molten hot. I threw it on the ground near the orc's head.

"Don't do that!" yelled Warren. "If that's a gate key, he might be able to use it!"

As one, the entire crew—even Harvey—turned to look at Warren as if he were a complete moron.

"I'm pretty sure he's more than just a bit dead, Warren," I stated.

In return, Warren squinted, looked over at Trezgel, and then looked down at his feet, muttering something under his breath.

The room flashed.

I covered my eyes just in time, but it was so bright that I saw spots for a couple of minutes following it. Plus, my head was ringing like we'd been hit with a concussion grenade.

"What just happened?" I asked as my ears began to clear.

Turbo pointed.

The key had melted into the floor.

"That's it, then," announced Griff. "The orc bodies we saw

in stasis have disintegrated. The key was the only thing keeping them intact."

"You're sure?" I asked pointedly.

"Positive."

If anyone would know, it'd be Griff. Of course, he was also the one who said our portal landing would be nice and cushy. It was not.

I wanted to stand up and get the hell out of here, but since the danger was gone, I just put my head back on the hardwood floor and shut my eyes. There was a lot to come to grips with over what had happened tonight.

"What do we do with the head?" asked Warren.

I probably should have had Lydia get Paula Rose and The Spin down here to check it out, but dealing with my ex right now honestly wasn't something I found all that enticing. Besides, it wasn't like anyone on the Strip was any the wiser of what had gone down tonight.

With a small grin, I answered, "I'd say the guy who got us all into this mess should be the one to clean it up."

"Right."

CHAPTER 46

The Directors were in surprisingly good spirits as I sat there before them. It seemed that EQK had been directed to go through sensitivity training after the other Directors had complained. They seemed pleased with themselves.

EQK hadn't gone already, obviously, but the very fact that it was on his schedule made everyone else happy.

"A dragon is definitely a rarity in the Overworld," said O. "I've not heard of one being allowed up since the breaking of the Badlands."

"Nor I," agreed Silver. "Clearly she snuck through somehow."

"They *are* tricky," agreed Zack. "Honestly, though, I'm more worried about the fact that there was an orc still alive." He hesitated. "Not that I'm fond of the concept of genocide. That's *not* my point. I'm speaking specifically in terms of the fact that none were supposed to have remained, and yet clearly one has…or had."

We sat in silence for a minute, mulling over things. I

didn't know a ton about the history of the Netherworld, but like most people, I knew the highlights.

Orcs were created by the dragons in order to battle against Netherworld Proper. They failed. The dragons went into hiding. The orcs kept coming. The dragons soon found themselves under attack from the very beasts they'd created, and so they teamed up with the rest of the Netherworld and a massive battle ensued. Many lives were lost as they sought to destroy every last orc.

It was a terrible time in Netherworld history.

"You guys are dicks," said EQK out of the blue. "Just because I happened to call O by his full name doesn't mean you should rat me out."

O slammed his hands on the desk. "My full name is *not* Osshole!"

"It isn't?"

"Why would you think it is?"

"Maybe your parents saw into the future and determined what kind of person you'd be?" EQK replied, sounding innocent.

"Not only does that make zero sense, EQK," O said in a tight voice, "it's insulting."

"Hmmm." The pixie was rarely stumped. "Well, then, I...apologize."

This stunned the room.

We'd just been discussing dragons and orcs and genocide, which should have been sobering enough, but an apology from EQK? That was just downright unprecedented.

"Seriously?" said Silver.

"Yeah, are you being for real?" asked Zack.

O leaned forward for a moment. "Is this an honest apology, EQK?"

"I..." It was clear the pixie was struggling. "Well..." He

cleared his throat and coughed a few times. "Ah, fuck it! No, it's not a real apology! I'll take the sensitivity training and piss all over the instructor. You guys are the Three Musketeers of douchebaggery! Osshole, Shitvers, and Crack!"

"Shitvers?"

"Crack?"

I tried not to laugh. Seriously, I tried. But it was no use.

"What are you laughing at, Wrong Sex Dex?" EQK snapped.

I sobered.

"Wrong Sex Dex?" I said, confused. "I don't get it."

"'Cause you're a woman in a man's body, dipshit."

"Clever," I said back, and then added something I probably shouldn't have. "That means very little coming from someone named EQGay."

There was a line that one didn't cross with their superiors, especially in the Paranormal Police Department. It was an imaginary border that rested between acceptable and unacceptable behavior. EQK crossed it with his peers all of the time, and it seemed he was finally going to be paying a penance for that, but for me to cross that line against the Directors was not good.

The room was dead silent.

It was in a moment like this when EQK was well within his rights to have my job yanked right out from under me.

I was sweating.

And then the pixie burst out laughing.

"EQGay!" he exclaimed through laughs. "I *love* it, WSD!"

"Who is WSD?" asked O.

"Wrong Sex Dex, Osshole," EQK said between laughs. "Don't you *ever* listen?"

I released a sigh of relief.

The others could reprimand me, but only EQK had the

right to put in a formal complaint since my insult was aimed at him.

Just in case, I said, "I'm sorry for my outburst, sirs." Then I adjusted in my chair and quickly moved to get the subject back on track. "Again, uh...the dragon has been destroyed, and the orcs, I'm told, are no more."

There was another few seconds of quiet.

"If the key was destroyed," agreed O finally, "that would be the end of them."

I nodded. "That's what Officer Benchley said as well, sir."

"I guess that's that, then," said Silver. "I have another appointment to attend to."

With that his station went dark.

"Me as well," stated Zack a moment before his area dimmed.

"Good job, Officer Dex," O said. "We will meet again soon."

That just left me and EQK.

"The EQGay thing was funny," admitted the pixie, "but if you do anything like that again, I'll have your nuts in a sling. Got it?"

"Got it."

"You're all right, Dex," he said, using my actual name. "These other guys are dicks, but you're more like me than they are. I dig that."

"Thank you...sir."

"Fuck off."

And with that, his station light went out.

hen I stepped out of the back room and into my office, I found Rachel seated in one of my guest chairs.

She had an envelope in her hand.

"Hey, Rachel," I said, somewhat surprised at seeing her there. I'd assumed she was still pissed off at me for having gotten laid in the circle of valkyries. "What's going on?"

In response, she set the envelope on the desk and pushed it toward me.

I opened it, but before I could even unfold the paper, she spoke up.

"I'm transferring to London."

It felt like someone had just punched me in the stomach.

I sat down.

"What?"

"I can't do it anymore, Ian," she said, not looking at me. "It's been years and I just can't let go."

"Of what?"

"You, you idiot," she answered in a huff. "And it's clear you don't feel the same way, so I'm leaving."

But I *did* feel the same way. I just couldn't do anything about it. I was her boss, for crying out loud!

"Rachel," I said, fighting to keep my voice calm, "you know how I feel about you, but you also know that we can't do anything about it right now."

"I'm well aware of the circumstances," she replied. "It's no longer worth discussing."

"If this is about me getting laid in the—"

"It has nothing to do with that, Ian," she replied and then groaned. "Okay, it has *something* to do with that, but not completely." She shut her eyes and took a deep breath. "It used to be okay because we were only fighting against other supernaturals. There'd be a rogue vampire here and there, or a werewolf who crapped on someone's yard, but now there are ubernaturals and you've been damn near next to dead more than once since they've come on to the scene."

"So have you," I replied. "Everyone has."

"I know that." Her response was heated. She held up her hands and repeated it more softly. "I know that. But this time we got separated. This time I was going through that hidden tunnel while you were all alone going through the nine levels. I couldn't do anything to help. I couldn't do anything to protect you." She was clearly on the verge of tears. "I can't allow that to happen again."

I flicked the edge of her letter.

"And so you think that by transferring to London you're going to somehow be able to better protect me?"

"No," she said, "but going there means that there is no more chance of us ever being together. That means I can start a new life. I can find someone...someone else." She looked away. "I can put what we had behind me."

I wanted to fight her. I wanted to tell her that this was all a bunch of bullshit. That none of this mattered.

But she was right.

"Have you told the others?" I asked after a few minutes of silence.

She stood up. "Yes."

I nodded as she walked from my office.

CHAPTER 48

*T*he drinks weren't quite strong enough tonight at the Three Angry Wives Pub. I had the feeling not much was going to quench my angst at the moment.

Rachel was gone from my crew.

I could have rushed after her, but I didn't. I needed to think about everything. There had been plenty of time over the last five years to figure out a way to make things work between us, but I never did it. Doing so now in some mad rush to save things made no sense.

Again, I needed to think.

"Ah, Mr. Dex," said Gabe as he took a seat across from me. He was the vampire who had brought the wonders of things like *Flashes* and *Time.* "Having a few extra drinks tonight, I see?"

"Rachel left the team," I replied.

He raised an eyebrow. "Officer Cress is gone?"

"You heard me, pal."

"Where did she go?"

The way he asked the question seemed a bit gruff. I regarded him for a moment, but he never broke eye contact.

"London PPD," I answered. "Why?"

He looked to be in thought for a moment.

"No reason," he said. Then he clasped his hands together. "Rumor has it your team was able to take down a dragon by the name of Charlotte."

"How would you know that?"

"So the rumors are true, then," he said while signaling the waiter to bring him a drink. "That's a difficult task."

"It wasn't a lot of fun."

"Did you use *Time* to assist you?"

I squeezed down the rest of my whiskey and nodded.

"Used it twice, actually."

His head jolted. "Twice?"

"Yeah, once while boning my psyc—" I paused and looked up. "I mean, I used it during sex with this chick I know. Extended her orgasm in my world." Then I shrugged. "The other time was to stop the dragon from tearing a hole in the fabric of reality or some shit."

The waiter dropped off two more drinks, one for me and the other for Gabe. The vampire sipped at his. Mine didn't last long.

"You *do* realize that you only have three uses of *Time?*"

I glared.

"No, Gabe," I said pointedly, "I *didn't* know that. And you wanna know why I didn't know that?" I didn't wait for a response. "I didn't know that because you never fucking told me that!"

"Calm down, calm down," he said, waving his hands at me. "Just be super careful with how you choose to use it the last time." He then took another sip and added, "Sorry about losing your partner."

I grunted in response and put my head on the table.

Usually I talked to Rachel about things that went bad in my life. Who was I going to talk to now? Gabe? Nah. I barely knew the guy. Dr. Vernon was an option, but only if I stopped boning her. Seeing that I had the valkyries at my disposal now, I could go back to keeping my psychology appointments professional. That probably wouldn't go over very well, though.

Man, my dick sure did get me into a lot of trouble.

With a groan, I said, "Why are you giving me these special abilities anyway?"

He pushed back from the table and stood up.

"Until next time, Mr. Dex," he said. Then he paused. "Please be more careful with the items I give you to work with. They are not to be used recklessly."

I sat up and gave him a sour look.

"Also," he added, "I believe that you will somehow *Sniff* your way out of this predicament you have with your former partner."

Sniff?

"That sounds wrong, dude."

He paused and chewed his lip. "Yes, I suppose it does. Regardless, use it wisely."

As I sat there pondering life, thinking about what was next, and wondering what the hell *Sniff* would do for me, I blew out a long breath while allowing my lips to vibrate.

"I guess I could take Harvey under my wing for a while and teach him the ropes," I said to the empty glass of whiskey in front of me.

My mind drifted back to Rachel and I signaled for another shot of pain reduction.

It was going to be a long night.

Thanks for Reading

If you enjoyed this book, would you please leave a review at the site you purchased it from? It doesn't have to be a book report... just a line or two would be fantastic and it would really help us out!

John P. Logsdon
www.JohnPLogsdon.com

John was raised in the MD/VA/DC area. Growing up, John had a steady interest in writing stories, playing music, and tinkering with computers. He spent over 20 years working in the video games industry where he acted as designer and producer on many online games. He's written science fiction, fantasy, humor, and even books on game development. While he enjoys writing lighthearted adventures and wacky comedies most, he can't seem to turn down writing darker fiction. John lives with his wife, son, and Chihuahua.

Christopher P. Young

Chris grew up in the Maryland suburbs. He spent the majority of his childhood reading and writing science fiction and learning the craft of storytelling. He worked as a designer and producer in the video games industry for a number of years as well as working in technology and admin services. He enjoys writing both serious and comedic science fiction and fantasy. Chris lives with his wife and an ever-growing population of critters.

CRIMSON MYTH PRESS

Crimson Myth Press offers more books by this author as well as books from a few other hand-picked authors. From science fiction & fantasy to adventure & mystery, we bring the best stories for adults and kids alike.

www.CrimsonMyth.com

Made in the USA
Middletown, DE
02 December 2019